Jigsaw

Teresa Adele Bettino

Jigsaw by Teresa Adele Bettino

Cover: Courtesy Lucy Roehm

Cover Design: Lucy Roehm

ISBN: 978-0-9742842-5-5

Lucy Roehm

Lucy Roehm is a self-taught artist who has taken many classes and workshops in the Philadelphia area. She has always had an interest in art, but did not start painting until the fall of 1997. Her first art classes were at the Cheltenham Township Adult School with Gwen Koths. She continued these weekly classes through the spring of 2001. She attributes much of what she learned and her improved technique in painting to these weekly classes.

Lucy also studied graphite and colored pencil with Eileen Rosen at Morris Arboretum in Philadelphia. This was a wonderful learning experience and Lucy realized how much she enjoyed botanical drawing and creating miniature landscapes with colored pencil. Colored pencil and graphite continues to be one of her favorite media.

Lucy started painting with watercolors in 2003 by attending classes at Tamanend Park, taught by a prominent Buck's county artist, Joan Feiss. Lucy attended local watercolor classes with prominent Philadelphia watercolorist, Howard Watson. Following these classes, in May, 2005 she attended a weeklong workshop with nationally recognized watercolor artist, Tony Couch. This workshop proved to be one of Lucy's most valuable learning experiences for watercolor technique and use of color. Lucy currently attends workshops with collage and watercolor artist, Alice Meyer-Wallace at the Plastic Club in Philadelphia. Lucy also attended a workshop in Spain with Alice in September, 2009.

Lucy started exhibiting her paintings in the spring of 2003. She has shown her work at Mixed Media Gallery in Doylestown, The Tinicum Arts Festival in Erwinna, PA, and local churches and libraries in Montgomery County, PA. Other exhibits include, the Church of the Holy Trinity, the Plastic Club, the Philadelphia

Sketch Club, the Cosmopolitan Club, Newman Galleries, and Woodmere Art Museum, all in Philadelphia. In May, 2009, many of Lucy's paintings were displayed at the Paoli Hospital Cancer Center in Paoli, PA.

She has won awards for both her watercolor and oil paintings. Lucy had her first solo exhibit, "Seaside Dreams", at Gould Gallery on Third Street in Old City, Philadelphia in September, 2005, and exhibited her floral paintings there through March, 2006. She paints many landscapes on Chincoteague Island Virginia, where she and her husband have a vacation home. The Linda Nerine Gallery in Chincoteague most recently represented her work. Lucy's paintings will now be on display at The Island Cottage on Maddox Boulevard on Chincoteague Island.

Lucy is a member of the Oreland Art Center, the Plastic Club, Philadelphia Sketch Club, and Woodmere Art Museum.

After working for many years as a medical technologist, the artist retired in 2007, and now devotes more time to painting and her art career. Lucy and her husband Ron, also retired, enjoy spending more time in Chincoteague, Virginia. Their interests include antiquing, classic cars, and travel. They live in Elkins Park, PA with their two cats Spike and Polly.

There is no warning for upcoming danger.

(Cheyenne)

Dedication

Liz Spino

A chance meeting on Assateague...

Chincoteague Island, Virginia

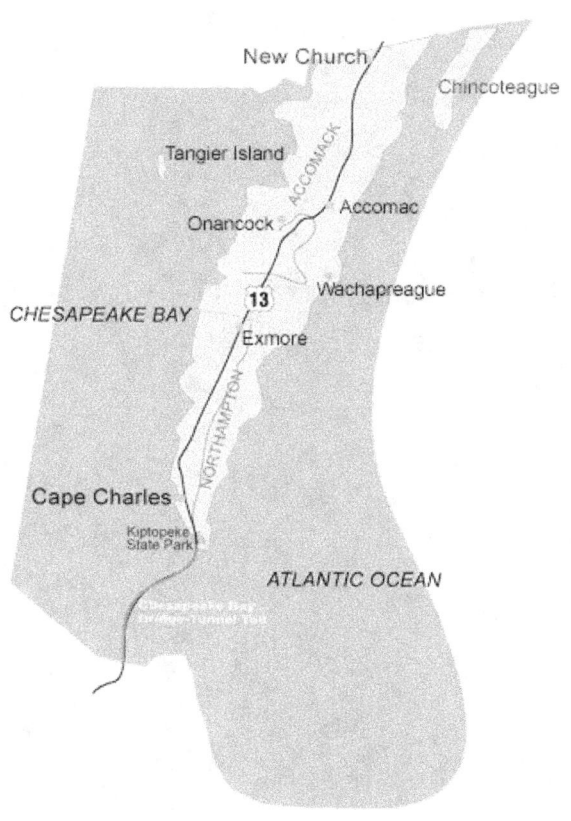

Virginia Eastern Shore

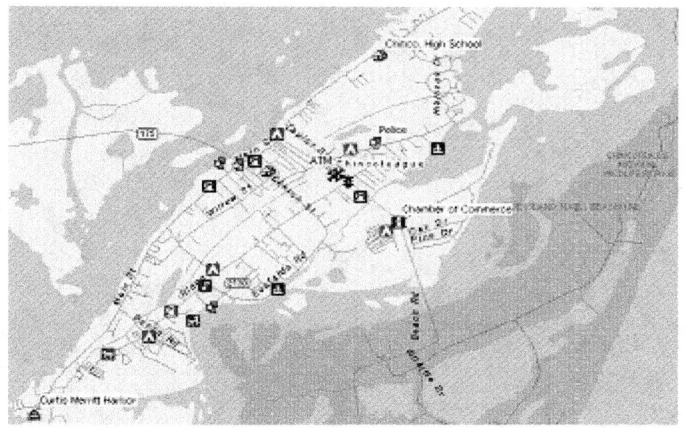

Jigsaw

Teresa Adele Bettino

1

It's not hot, foggy, buggy, rainy or Monday, the day of the week that I dread. It's Tuesday and it's snowing on the Eastern Shore of Virginia. I'm on-call for child and adult abuse and snow isn't a good sign. Life stops with the first speck of snow. Before the flake hits the frozen ground, schools are closed; bread and milk in grocery stores don't exist and forget about finding cat litter. God forbid that anybody has an indoor cat and needs to change their cat's litter box.

Life stopping doesn't mean that everybody enjoys a good snowstorm. Folks lose patience, smack their kids and abuse elderly. When bad weather hits, kids get bored, parents get cabin fever and calls to the State Hot Line begin. That's when I become busy. I investigate abuse reports.

I'm Francie Batista and am employed by the Virginia Department of Social Services. I live on Chincoteague Island, a barrier island, which is a tiny spot on the Eastern Shore. I've read somewhere that the island's about thirty-seven square miles and only nine square miles is land. My office is located in the back portion of an undersized recently painted building between Sundial Books and the renovated library, located on Main Street. Although my office is cluttered and cramped, it has a fantastic view of the park and the Chincoteague Bay. This agency is considered a satellite office with the main social service agency located about twenty minutes south. I'm the only social worker here, which affords me some kudos, like bringing my two rescue dogs, Sergeant and Bella to work.

There's a recently hired male eligibility worker, Chip Wells that shares the office with me. He serves as a receptionist and is also an eligibility worker who approves food stamps and Medicaid applications. Chip was hired two months ago. The previous worker, Wanda Burton, had a severe melt down and never returned. Her new residence is Central State Hospital. Wanda was found not guilty of trying to kill her uncle, Lou Mann, in the reception area of the agency last year, during the time when a killer was running loose on the island. Wanda's insane, and hated her job, so it's a blessing that she isn't returning. When she and I worked together we were supposed to be a supportive team. Wanda and I didn't communicate. To be honest, I was scared of her. She would sit at her desk and glare at me. The environment of the office was hostile, even though a hostile work environment usually has something to do with sex. This didn't. I called it fearing for my life and labeled this environment as hostile.

Since Chip was hired, there's been a surge of females coming to the agency to apply for benefits. They sit in the waiting room, polishing their nails, putting on make-up, and socializing. Chip has the appearance of Jacob Black, from *The Twilight Saga*. I'm not implying that he's a werewolf. Although, similar to Jacob whose Native American; Chip says that he's a descendent of Laughing King, who was a peaceful Eastern Shore Accomack Native American. Chip works out daily, has a six-pack stomach, long dark flowing, thick straight hair and howls with my dogs every time a siren goes off on the island.

This snow has me nervous. I know that within a twenty-four hour period that I'll be receiving numerous reports. I'm sitting at my desk, continuing to feel pathetic, reading *The Washington Post*. There's a front-page article about a photographer, Frances Benjamin Johnston, who took a bunch of pictures of the Eastern Shore during the 1930's. Some low life's broken into the Library of Congress and stole her stuff.

I place the paper down on my littered desk and look out the window. Sea Gulls have collected on the fishing pier and are, facing the Chincoteague Bay, feathers puffed with heads tucked under their wings. Chip hasn't arrived. I'm depressed, there's no two ways about it. Depression is bad…zaps energy and life. Why was I born in this dreary month of December? The sun hardly shines, the weather's cold and even though Christmas is ten days away, I don't care. I haven't purchased one gift. I've diagnosed myself with Affective Seasonal Disorder. Some professionals call it a mood disorder. My symptoms include overeating, especially carbohydrates, and withdrawal from friends. To add to my general negative spirit, I'm on-call over Christmas week including New Years Eve.

The bell hanging on the front door jingles bringing my mind back to the present. Somebody's walked in and needs some services. I quickly roll my chair back, trampling over some cases that I have thrown onto the floor. Now there's black wheel marks across two of my cases.

Sergeant and Bella follow me to the reception area and we see Jodi Burgess. I hear some giggling and the dogs give a friendly bark.

"Where's Francie Batista, the birthday girl?" Jodi says chuckling, as she shakes a white bag.

Sugarbakers, a local bakery has the best doughnuts on the island. Jodi hands me the bag and I take a peek. Two sugar jelly doughnuts still warm; my mood's suddenly shifting.

Investigator Jodi Burgess saved my life about a year ago when she was a sheriff's investigator living on the island. She's my best friend. Jodi and I worked many investigations together, but one in particular we will never forget. This psycho-murderer moved from Maryland to Watts Estates, located on the mainland near Wallops Island, and started killing folks including a horse at the barn where I have my horse, Trooper, boarded. Bart Connors became known as The Eastern Shore Wind Chime Killer, as he attached a horse wind chime to his victims. He followed Jodi and me to Key West, Florida on our vacation. I guess Bart had a grudge against social workers stemming from his troubled childhood and attempted to reduce the number. I ended up getting a bullet to my shoulder and he ended up dead. After we returned to Chincoteague, Jodi relocated to the mainland, and was promoted to sergeant of the Cold Case Unit in Norfolk.

"Jodi, I can't believe that you remembered my birthday."

"Of course, I remembered...twenty-five and do you believe all of this snow. I love it!"

I begin to eat a jelly doughnut and gulp a flat warm soda to wash it down. "You can't be serious. I hate snow."

"I know, girlfriend. We need to plan a get-away trip to the Florida Keys again."

"No thanks. The last get-away we did, I almost died. And I don't ever want to see the Keys again."

"What are you doing in Chincoteague?"

"I have a surprise. It hasn't been announced yet, so don't tell anyone especially your mother."

I roll my eyes and smile. Jodi has always trusted me with secrets. She's really close to my mother, Gertrude, a retired social worker, who lives near Charlottesville, about a five-hour drive, west.

"OK, tell me."

"I'm living in Chincoteague again and begin work on Monday as captain of the sheriff's department. I applied for Captain Harold Winston's job, interviewed, and got the position."

Captain Harold Winston retired in glory after The Eastern Shore Wind Chime Killer was no more. He still lives in Chincoteague, "down the island" not far from Curtis Merritt Harbor. His wife, Ginger has been doing volunteer work at the library and visits Sergeant and Bella a couple of times a week. Sometimes when I need to leave the agency and my co-worker, Chip isn't available, Ginger dog-sits.

"Oh my God, that's great... fantastic. I can't imagine you as captain. Will you be able to go out on investigations with me, like old times, or are you going to grow old, behind your desk working endlessly on paperwork?" I say without a smile.

"Francie, at times you're so much fun to be around and other times you are really unpleasant. Of course, periodically we'll work together, like old times. I'm so glad to be back. I really didn't like living in Norfolk. I didn't make any friends and missed living on an island. There weren't any ducks to watch crossing the street and I didn't have anyone to pal around with."

"I'm sorry that I'm being negative. It's just that I hate this time of the year. I feel like there's much negative energy surrounding me. Remember, when I get a chill running up and

16

down my spine and how I feel that something horrible is going to happen? Do you recall last year when I kept telling you that I felt a chill running, up my spine, and that my Italian grandmother used to say, "Somebody's just walked over my grave!" Every time I feel that shiver, something horrendous happens."

"Calm down Francie. You're getting all worked up. We're just having a little bit of snow. No big deal. It will be over by noon. Why don't you hang the Out of Office sign on the door, and we'll walk down the block to visit Jon and Jane at Sundial Books. I bet they would like a visit from Sergeant and Bella too, especially Jon as he loves to throw the tennis ball to Sergeant."

I place the Out of Office sign on the front door, throw a brown shawl over my shoulders and pull on a pair of mucking boots. I love my shawl as Mom knitted it for me last Christmas. I wear it every day in the winter. I also have a fondness for my mucking boots. I wear them to work, mucking stalls and horseback riding.

Sergeant and Bella eager to leave and play in the snow, begin to jump around Jodi and me as we proceed onto Main Street. It's about nine in the morning and already snow is covering the sidewalks. We yell across the street to Kaylee, a volunteer with Chincoteague Animal Rescue. Yelling "Hello" she turns to wave and slips, falling onto the sidewalk. Jodi and I cross the street with Sergeant and Bella. They're enjoying the snow, dashing and placing their noses into it for some winter pleasure. Kaylee was holding a grocery bag prior to her fall. The contents of the bag scatter and cat food cans roll onto Main Street. Kaylee has a feeding station for the island's feral cats behind the Village Mall. She owns a small antique shop on the back left side of the building. I acquired Sergeant, a Shepherd mix and Bella, a Pit-Bull mix, from her last year when the killer was on the loose. Sergeant and Bella saved me, when somebody entered my apartment on our first night together as a family.

Just as I bend to offer a hand, Bella runs into me knocking me off balance. I fall narrowly missing Kaylee. Kaylee laughs at

Bella's antics, and Jodi offers us her hands. Kaylee and I look at one another, smile and pull Jodi off balance. She falls between us as the dogs run in circles. Jon, who's at the corner throwing salt, in front of his store, Sundial Books, hears the commotion. He crosses Main Street and offers a hand to Jodi.

"I didn't know that you had returned from Norfolk. Glad to see you Jodi."

"Today's Francie's birthday, so I came to surprise her." Jodi says smiling as she wipes snow from her jeans and brown leather jacket.

"Here's a hand-up, Francie and one for you Kaylee."

Sergeant and Bella hear the door open at Sundial Books and run wildly across the street to Jane as she steps outside the store looking for Jon.

"There you are. I wondered what happened to you. I guess the front of the mall needs some salt also from the looks of it. I'll watch the dogs if it's alright with you Francie. You know Tuesday's are our special day."

Tuesdays are story time for island youngsters. The dogs visit every Tuesday morning to play with little ones, listen to stories, get petted and eat treats. I don't know if story time will happen today as there's no life moving on Main Street. Folks aren't even drinking coffee from Sugarbakers or Main Street Coffeehouse. There's been no let up with this snow. I've just noticed that the wind's shifted from Chincoteague Bay. It's blowing from the south. Southern storms are the worst.

Jodi and I walk across the street to Sundial Books as Kaylee enters the mall. Jon continues to throw salt. I look up and notice that the clouds are gray. No gulls are flying, and the island ducks aren't around. Not a good sign.

Park Ranger Molly Smith enters Assateague Island National Seashore. The snow has covered sea grasses and roads. She's cold; the temperature is below freezing and the wind's blowing.

Her nostrils are frozen and snow's gathering onto her face. Her scarf isn't helping. She hasn't dressed for the weather and is disappointed with herself that she didn't plan ahead. No gloves or ski mask. She's wearing a light jacket with her park ranger hat, which offers little protection, as her short fine hair is wet and icy. She's shivering. She rubs her hands together and blows her breath onto them. Having been raised in Boston and a park ranger at the Grand Canyon, Molly considers herself seasoned, although the magnitude of this storm has taken her by surprise.

Molly's new to the Commonwealth. She was hired shortly after the murder of Ranger Maureen Hughes and the untimely death of Ranger Tony Jarrett. Maureen was killed by Bart Connors. Tony committed suicide shortly after discovering Maureen executed, sitting inside of the ranger's station. After learning of where Maureen was murdered, Molly doesn't hang about the station. She finds this depressing. Molly enjoys roaming the park, speaking with visitors, observing the migration of birds and watching wild ponies. She loves the ocean and southern hospitality.

The weather's of concern; high winds are causing a whiteout to ensue. This cold, snowy, dreary day is atypical and Molly's apprehensive as to the welfare of the ponies.

Molly's been busy learning about equines. As a child, she didn't have an opportunity to own or to ride horses. At the end of the summer when the state fair came to Massachusetts, she watched horse shows, dreaming of the day when she would learn how to ride a horse and maybe own one. Molly's first love was a Shetland pony named Daisy. She watched Daisy entertain children while penned at the fair. Molly learned that Shetland ponies originated on the Shetland Islands, a little north of Scotland. Shetland ponies, a sturdy breed, are accustomed to harsh winters. When Molly transferred to Assateague, she read about Chincoteague ponies, which have similar qualities. They are sturdy and survive living on sea grasses and pond waters. Of course the first book that Molly read after transferring to

Assateague was Marguerite Henry's *Misty of Chincoteague*, a must for any Assateague park ranger.

Molly loves observing Chincoteague ponies. She follows them throughout the day and knows their habits. Mornings and late afternoons, Surfer Dude, a solid liver chestnut stallion, with a thick, long-flowing blond mane and tail, is seen grazing at Tom's Cove, with his mares, Virginia Belle and Gone with the Wind.

Another stallion, Miracle Man, a Pinto, may be a descendent from Spanish horses, which were transported to America during the sixteenth century. Perhaps the theory of a Spanish Galleon sinking off of Assateague has some merit. Miracle Man's eye-catching as he's distinguished from others with his bay, dark dot markings. Years ago, Native American's favored Pintos for their decorative coats as their coat provided camouflage while traveling in woods and mountain ranges. Although Assateague doesn't have mountain ranges, the island has woods and during the summer when foliage is full, Molly has difficulty spotting the Pinto.

Tom's Cove a grassy wetland offers nutritional grazing for the ponies. It's a short distance to the Pony Corral, where Salt Water Cowboys, many members of the Chincoteague Fire Department, round up ponies. This was Molly's first July and she enjoyed observing the ponies swim across Assateague Inlet. She learned that the first foal to reach the shore is named King or Queen Neptune and is raffled off. Some lucky individual wins a foal. Thousands of tourists come to the island to witness history. It's a two-day celebration. The money made from the auction provides revenue for the fire department and serves to decrease the bands of ponies roaming Assateague.

Molly's hopeful to complete a head count and uses her new 4-wheel drive, black Ford. She pulls over to the right shoulder, opens the driver's door, grabs her coffee cup and takes a swig. Her binoculars are hanging around her neck. She's hopeful to see a band of ponies and doesn't. Molly continues with her mission. She returns to her vehicle and arrives at the Pony

Corral. She parks and walks the path to the corral. It's slippery and she falls, losing her cell phone in a drift. She recovers it although her fingers are frozen as she grips her binoculars bringing them to her eyes...searching. Molly sees movement, focuses and determines that Witchdoctor's moving around near the corral. He's, the oldest stallion. Witchdoctor's prancing, snorting; his behavior is out of the ordinary and Molly's trying to figure out what the hell is going on. Using the zoom lenses of her binoculars she drifts her eyes to the corral, and sees four foals inside the of the pen, with their heads hanging nearly to the snow covered ground, not moving.

2

Sergeant and Bella are the only audience for story time. Jane's reading Noel Tennyson's children's story, *The Lady's Chair* as Jodi and I enter Sundial Books just in time to listen to Jane saying, "It was one of those rooms, all flowery and soft, like the kind grandmothers have, and in one corner, under a south window, there was a chair. It was a high-backed wing chair called a lady's chair."

As Jodi and I settle into the wicker chairs located in the back portion of the store, we listen as Jane continues. The snow's ominous; sky dreary with fishing boats swaying back and forth tied to the dock. "The lady's chair belonged to Mrs. Seddi Hopewell. It was her favorite chair, the one she read in and did her knitting in, and the one in which she had her afternoon tea." Bella's snoring to the rhythm of Jane's tender voice as Sergeant sits directly in front of Jane wagging her tail.

Just as Jane ends with the word tea, a siren goes off and Jodi and I walk to the front of the store and look out windows facing Main Street. Sammy's driving the only snowplow in Chincoteague, with Salt Water Cowboys, trailing behind driving their trucks, traveling north on Main. We open the door and step out into the elements. The snowplow and convoy make a right onto Maddox. The siren sounding causes Sergeant and Bella to howl, interrupting story time.

"So much for story time Jodi. I really need to get back to the agency. It's been good seeing you. When can I tell mom the news?"

"Tomorrow during staff meeting the acting captain will announce that Captain Harold Winston's vacant position has been filled, so I'll give you a call right after the meeting's over."

"OK. I can't wait to work with you again and to see you more often."

Jodi and I wait a moment for Jane to complete the next sentence. The dogs hear and see me open the front door and know that it's time to leave. As we head back to the agency, Jon's throwing salt onto the sidewalk in front of Roxy Theater. He's all wet. I wave to Jon and say "good-bye" to Jodi as I enter the agency with Sergeant and Bella at my heels.

The waiting room's packed with women. Chip Wells has arrived and is beginning his day of intake. Everybody's taken a number and is waiting patiently. Hair has been washed, nails polished and make-up is on.

"Francie, before you go to your office, you've received three reports from the State Hot Line and you have, Abby Soloman waiting to talk with you about her grandmother."

"Alright. If you can inform Ms. Soloman that I will be with her in a minute, I'd appreciate it." I walk over to the fax machine and retrieve the reports. Sergeant and Bella follow me to my office and are ready for naptime. I quickly review the three reports, two of which are child protective service reports and one's an adult neglect report.

I walk to the reception area and call Abby Soloman's name. She's sitting in the corner absorbed reading *a People Magazine*. Ms. Soloman follows me to my office.

"Hello Ms. Soloman. I'm Francie Batista. I understand that you want to speak with me about your grandmother."

"Yes, I do. Can we shut your door as this is a very private matter and I don't want my friends hearing anything about what I'm about to tell you."

Oh God...this has an element of additional Francie stress for the morning...it's going to be a good one...I can sense it... for this lady to arrive during a major snowstorm. I feel as though I need a drink, fat marijuana joint and lots of chocolate.

I walk over to the door; give Chip a wink, as I shut my office door. I walk to my desk, and sit down. I have a pad of paper and an adult protective service form to write on if necessary.

"Ms. Batista. My grandmother is Carry Sadie Nation-Savage, as she was named after women who whole-heartedly believed in not drinking, not smoking, no sex prior to marriage and were deeply religious.

Boy, I can tell that this is going to be a long one...probably two feet of snow will fall prior to Ms. Soloman getting to the chase.

"Excuse me Ms. Soloman, would you like to have a cup of hot tea and a chocolate granola bar?"

"Yes, honey.   That would be good.   I do like granola, although never have had chocolate on it.   I would like some lemon in my tea."

I push my chair back, running over cases again, and trip on the telephone cord, stumbling to the kitchen.

"I'll be right with you, Ms. Soloman."

"That's fine. And you can call me Abby."

I think that it's fair to say that this is going to be an all day affair with Abby.   Maybe the agency will catch on fire so that I can get rid of her.

"Abby, I'm coming with your tea and granola." I hand Abby her tea with a slice of lemon and granola, take my coffee mug and chug it.

"You were saying that your grandmother was named after two righteous women."

"Yes, you see Ms. Batista; my grandmother raised me and lives in Temperanceville, not far from Conquest Chapel. Cary A. Nation traveled around preaching righteousness, emptying liquor bottles and bars with patrons across our nation. At one time she came to the Eastern Shore to speak about the ills of living in sin, so to speak. The other woman that my grandmother is named after is Sadie Savage, who grew up in a small eastern shore community named Onley. Sadie Savage and Cary Nation were strong supporters of the temperance movement. It all had to do with prohibition. *Alright, history 101...* Well, I'm married now and moved away about ten years ago. I keep in touch weekly with my grandmother. *This is really moving slowly...I stretch and look out of the window. There's a fat, snow covered duck, with his head tucked under his wing, sitting on the dock.* Anyway, Ms. Batista...do you know any of the popular porno stars making movies these days?"

What the! My coffee spills onto the folders located on the floor that I have run over twice today.

"Excuse me Abby, did I hear you correctly?"

"Yes, Ms. Batista you did hear me correctly."

"Abby, you can call me Francie.

"Alright, honey. There's a man, Ron Jeremy, who stars in porno movies. He made a movie called, *Bodacious Ta Ta's* in about 1980 and another one of his movies is, *Fun in a Bun.* I think that he made that movie in 1990."

This woman is nuts...

"Anyway for the past month or so when I call grandmother she tells me that she acted with Ron Jeremy. I think that my grandmother's demented. Francie, I know for a fact that my grandmother's innocent as she's a *God fearing woman.* How she ever came up with this guy's name is beyond me."

I shift in my chair and lean onto the desk for some physical support. "I can tell that you are really upset about this Ms. Soloman, um...Abby and what I will do is visit with your grandmother and assess her mental health status. It could be that she may have a nutritional problem or may have the beginning stages of memory problems. *I don't want to use the words demented or Alzheimer's and have Abby freak.* Now if you can give me Carry Sadie Nation-Savage's address that would suffice."

I escort Ms. Soloman through the reception area and out the front door. She's still clutching the *People Magazine* as she turns and waves good-bye.

I walk back to my office passing Chip and ask him not to disturb me for a few moments. Once back in my office, I Google the name Ron Jeremy. The State system icon pops directing me to go off this site, as it isn't work related. *No shit, Sherlock.* I'll give my supervisor, Paul Housemen a call and explain once I validate if this guy, Ron Jeremy is a porno star. *Bing, Bang, Bong...*there he is! Ron Jeremy is indeed a porno actor. He's been in the business since about 1970. Ron was a special education teacher, in which he received his

Masters...*wow*. He has acted in many films, over 1700 films and he's popular. Ron has the nickname, "The Hedgehog" from almost freezing to death while riding his motorcycle in shorts. He played in *Bodacious Ta Ta's* and *Fun in a Bun*. Ron has a large slong over nine inches worth; an envy of every young schmuck tongue bunging in the back seat of daddy's car. Maybe Carrie Sadie Nation-Savage knows Ron and did have an acting part. *I need something crunchy, as this is too much. Ah, there are some potato chips in my right bottom desk drawer. Who cares how long the chips have been there.*

I review the two child protective service reports and decide to go out on these. The adult report can wait until tomorrow. It's a self-neglect report as the aged male isn't bathing. Nobody's ever died from not bathing.

I open the door and give a large grin to Chip. The waiting room's packed. It's standing room only. Chip doesn't appear to be stressed with clients waiting. I peer into the reception area and spot Kaylee. She waves and I motion her to follow me.

Once inside of my office, I shut the door.

"Hey, what's up, Kaylee."

"I meant to speak with you this morning, but with falling and Jodi there I decided not to."

"Is there something wrong?" I ask reaching for another potato chip.

"No, it is just...I don't know how to ask you this, so I'll just say it. I would like for you to introduce me to Chip Wells. He is so good looking, and appears to have a good personality and you know as well as I that there's a shortage of good looking, intelligent young men on the island."

I take a deep breath and roll my eyes. Kaylee's a real sweetie. She's an all American gal, loves animals and wouldn't hurt a flea. "Kaylee, I'm trying to think of a way to introduce you, without making it look obvious. Can I think about it? Chip's a really nice person, hard working and friendly; I don't

JIGSAW Teresa Adele Bettino

know him though. Have you ever thought about asking him to
adopt a cat or a dog?"

"I was thinking of that. I said *Hello* to him the other day at
Bill's Restaurant. We were sitting in separate booths, eating
alone. I should have asked him to join me. I just didn't know if
that was proper or not."

"Oh...Kaylee, forget proper! He's probably just as shy as
you. Let me think of how to get you guys to meet and I'll get
back with you in a couple of days."

Kaylee and I proceed through the agency. She holds her head
down as she walks by Chip, too shy and embarrassed to look up.
I smile at Chip and escort Kaylee from the agency. I open the
front door and I'm in total shock. The snow's a total whiteout
and is now about knee high. A chill runs up and down my spine
as I quickly close the agency's door.

3

Doug Fields, a Salt Water Cowboy, is reading the *Chincoteague Beachcomber* newspaper and having his second cup of coffee. His wife Norma is traveling home from the chicken factory in Temperanceville as she works the midnight shift. He's concerned as the factory is about thirty minutes south and Norma's not a good driver, isn't used to driving in snow and has had her share of fender benders.

As he reaches for his coffee, Doug's cell phone rings and he places the paper on the kitchen table.

"Is this Doug Fields?"

"Yes."

"Mr. Fields, this is Ranger Molly Smith and we have a *major* situation here at the corral."

Doug looks at his watch, stares out the window and takes a sip of his coffee. He needs a cigarette. "What's the matter?"

"There are four close to death foals standing in the pen."

"What!"

"Yes, I was checking about the island, saw Witchdoctor prancing around the Pony Corral and like I said there are four very young foals freezing to death."

"OK. I'll be there in a few minutes." *Shit. What's going on?*

Doug walks over to the landline and calls the fire department. Russ Trotter the local blacksmith answers the phone.

"Yeah, what's up, Doug?"

"We've got a major problem with the ponies in Assateague. Sound the siren and get as many men as possible to meet at the Pony Corral. We need a stock trailer."

Within minutes, Doug's traveling to Assateague in his white Toyota and in the distance hears sirens. He drives down Chicken City Road and turns left onto Beach Road heading for the national park. He passes the vacant ranger station on his left, barely able to see it. Doug continues at a good pace, sees Molly's Ford and parks behind it. He opens the door and jumps out making his way down the path to the corral. He hears the only snowplow in Chincoteague pull up. Two cowboys get out, Russ and Sammy White, who works for the department of transportation. He's in charge of snow removal. Mike Griffin pulls up with a stock trailer and walks quickly to the path.

Ranger Smith meets the men half way and signals for them to move it. Mike and Sammy run to the corral, Doug and Russ walk quickly with their shoulders up and heads down.

Molly's covered with snow, and is shivering, "Please hurry," she says turning and sprinting as Mike and Sammy follow. All reach the pen, are staring and deep in thought. The foals appear to be a couple of days old.

Doug quickly takes charge.

"Mike, do you think that we can get the trailer down here without getting stuck in this damn snow? Does anybody know anyone that has mares lactating? I know Beth Keller and we can use a nanny goat if push comes to shove? We need to move fast here and figure the whys later."

Mike jogs away, up the snowy path for his truck.

Doug calls his wife, Norma. She should be at home by now and answers the landline. "Norma there's a situation up here at the corral in Assateague and it's an emergency. I know that you are friends with Beth Keller and Elizabeth Allen. Give Elizabeth and Beth a call. I'm looking for a couple of mares that have milk. If nobody has a couple of mares then we will need Beth's goats."

"What's going on?"

"I don't have time to explain but four foals are half dead, abandoned at the Pony Corral."

"OK. I'll call Beth and Elizabeth and get back with you."

Mike attempts to back the trailer down the path, however; it's too narrow and the trailer's pitching. He doesn't want to get stuck. He pulls out of the path, steps from his truck, leaving it idling. He watches as Sammy makes his way to the snowplow.

"Sam the plow needs to go down the path. I'll follow."

Sammy begins plowing a path, taking small trees and sea grass with him as he proceeds towards the Pony Corral. Mike moves forward with his truck pulling the stock trailer following Sam's cleared area. He's concentrating not to slide away from the plowed section. Mike's able to turn a bit, just enough to get the back of the trailer facing the gate of the pen. Russ and Doug are already in the pen with the foals gently petting and speaking to them. Molly's anxiously watching; she's still shaking from the cold.

Mike gets out of his truck, leaving it in neutral. Sammy turns off the plow's engine. Both young men are in their prime...working out daily at the local gym and they hop the pen fence with their legs out to the side like vaulting a gym horse, effortless. Mike and Sammy help Russ and Doug walk the foals into the stock trailer. The foals are easy to maneuver, as they're weak. The men hold onto the foal's manes as they place their other arm around the foal's hind quarters, and gently nudge each foal forward.

Once all are safely inside the trailer, Sammy jogs to the snowplow and uses the plow to push some snow out of the way so that Mike has access to a cleared path and road. Russ, Doug and Molly walk behind the trailer to the road. Molly's freezing and quickly jumps into her truck. She leans over and cranks the heat. Russ and Doug stop walking as their cell phones ring simultaneously.

"Yeah, hopefully you have some good news," Russ says as he shakes some of the snow from his hair, which is frozen and white.

"OK, thanks a lot, I'll tell Doug."

"Good news from Norma. We'll bring the foals in the next hour." Doug says as he walks swiftly to Mike. Russ smiles as he was going to say, "Head to Elizabeth Allen's farm."

"Mike, take the foals to Elizabeth Allen's farm. Beth has nanny goats and Elizabeth has a mare that recently lost her foal. Mike you do know where Watts Estates is?" Mike nods.

Doug walks over to Molly.

"Molly thanks for calling. Keep a look out. I don't understand any of this. These are not Chincoteague foals…no way…somebody's put these poor fellows here."

"I'll call in a few hours to see how things are. I'm going home to get warm…a change of clothes. I'll follow Sam out of here."

Sammy leads the way with Russ catching a ride with Mike. Doug's last. *Damn this weather, damn the person who did this, and damn I need a cigarette.*

Everybody's following Sammy's snowplow away from Assateague Island National Seashore. Doug is tailgating Mike. He can't see the foals only the back end of the stock trailer. Drifts are forming and the biting winds are kicking. Passing Tom's Cove is intimidating; as this whiteout is closing in on Doug making him feel claustrophobic. He needs some air to fill his lungs. What he really wants to fill his lungs is smoke from a cigarette, Camel to be exact.

The winds howl like a pack of wolves and as Molly hears howling winds for a moment she thinks she's at the Grand Canyon. She opens her window and looks out at Tom's Cove. On the side of the road walking towards the visitor center is Witchdoctor. She stares in disbelief. The convoy continues and she drives over the bridge, across Assateague Inlet and enters Chincoteague. Molly's clutching her steering wheel as she's stressed to the max and knows that she will not return to Assateague today. After passing the Oyster Museum, she leaves the caravan heading home towards Pine Drive.

4

It's lunchtime and the snow has continued. Knee deep to be exact and I have four reports to attend to. When it comes to child abuse and neglect, I attempt to have a face-to-face contact within a twenty-four hour period. I don't think that the county's dumpy Chevrolet will get me to where I need to go so I decide to call the Chincoteague Sheriff's Department for some help. Brittany's the contact person she's the administrative assistant for the captain and in this case the acting captain and transportation requests go to her. She's my contact person that I call for back up when necessary, which thank God doesn't happen that often.

Brittany was hired as an assistant to Chief Harold Winston and was about twenty years old when she gave a fantastic interview, by wearing a tight fitting knit dress, smiled at the Chief and obtained employment. With youthfulness, no wrinkles, style and having a set of knockers she was the most popular employee of the sheriff's department last year and still is. Brittany's just turned twenty-one, and is engaged, although being freshly engaged hasn't hurt her popularity with male deputies. Brit, can legally drink and enjoys drinking and meeting her boyfriend, Mike Griffin at the Village Restaurant. She's a very stylish dresser and I think that the Chief hired her to give him some life. She kept the captain motivated to show up for work. I wonder how Jodi and Brittany will get along. What's the expression, *two cooks in the kitchen, spoil what is it… the soup?*

I speed dial Brittany. She answers on the first ring.

"Hi, Brittany, this is Francie Batista, I was wondering if I could request some transportation assistance? I have four reports that I need to investigate. I don't feel safe driving the county's Chevy with this snow."

"I can request Deputy Greg Franks to transport you."

Oh no, how embarrassing. Greg's a transplant from New Mexico, speaks fluent Spanish, and worked a case with me. I haven't seen him since last year. The last memory I have of

Greg is doubled over gasping for air, holding a cell phone in one hand and a handkerchief in the other. I ran out of the Melton house holding a screaming baby as Mr. and Mrs. Melton had been positioned on their sofa, murdered, holding a horse wind chime. I was going to send Greg a thank you e-mail, for getting me into the home to retrieve the baby, however; never did, which is really ignorant of me. Oh well... I take a deep breath. "Yes, that would be fine. Thank you, Brittany."

Within ten minutes, Greg comes in through the back door of the agency. He's parked in the back lot. Snow is dripping from his hat.

"Hi, Greg. Nice to see you again."

"Don't mention it Francie. I figure that it's all in a day's job. What's up?"

I smile and get to the meat of the matter. "Greg, I have four reports, two child protective service reports and two adult protective service reports. The two adult reports can wait a day if we run out of time. With this whiteout, I don't feel comfortable driving."

"No problem." *This guy is too nice. I wonder if he is married.*

Prior to leaving, I inform Chip and give the dogs a chewy to keep them occupied so that they don't gnaw my case records from boredom. I grab my shawl and pull on my mucking boots. Out the back door we go as I hold my briefcase in one hand, and soda with the other.

"Greg, the first place that we're heading is on Booth Street not far from the Carnival Grounds. This child protective service complaint came in via the State Hot Line. The caller is anonymous, which I hate, as I can't call to ask questions or let the person know when I've reached a disposition. Maybe you know the family, Raymond and Mindy Robbins. They have a three year old daughter, Diane."

"No. I don't know this family."

"Well, anyway, the caller reported that Diane is covered with cigarette burns, especially on her buttocks. So I will need to take a look."

Greg pulls the snowy vehicle to the front of the Robbins home. The house appears well taken care of and has Christmas decorations, and lights framing the small Cape Cod, along with plastic reindeer; Santa is in the front yard smiling. I'm hopeful that they're at home. Where else would they be on a day like today?

Greg and I walk to the front door and he stands to the side as I knock. I give three hard knocks, wait and then knock again. The front wooden door opens slightly.

"Hello, um...Mindy Robbins. I am Francie Batista with social services and Deputy Greg Franks is with me due to the weather as I am unable to drive the agency vehicle. Can we come in?"

Mindy opens the door and permits access. The living room is neat, clean and odor free.

"Mrs. Robbins, do you have a three year old child named Diane?"

"Yes. What's this about? Does my husband need to be here? He's at work."

"No. I don't need to speak with your husband presently. *I hear Greg's breathing.* I am a child protective service worker, which means that I help families that may be having some parenting issues. I'm here because someone called and wanted me to check on Diane."

"What!" *I screwed up… it's too late to retract.*

"There's no reason to be alarmed. The department of social services receives many reports and it's my job to make sure that children as well as adults are OK. And if folks need help, it's my job to direct the family to receive appropriate services. The department gets many reports per year and I have to check the reports for validity. *I'm really over talking and need to shut up.* Is your daughter here?"

"Yes."

"How about if I go over the nature of the report with you and then I can visit with Diane as I will need to see her."

"I think that I need to call Ray and then call the family's attorney." *Shit.*

"Mrs. Robbins, if you feel as though you need to call your husband and your attorney, I can't prevent you from doing so, however; I believe that we can work together. Let me discuss with you the nature of the report."

"OK." *Thank God she's agreeable. There for a minute I thought that this was going downhill.*

"The nature of the report is that your daughter may have cigarette burns all over her body, so I will need to check her for burns and injury.

"Who in God's name would do a cruel joke like this? This is a waste of your time and my time Ms. Batista." Mindy says, walking away huffing and muttering under her breath.

Mindy leaves the living room and returns smiling as she holds her daughter, who appears clean and is dressed appropriately for the season. Her long sleeved T-shirt has a photo of Santa and her. Diane's pair of jeans has glitter on the pocket tops and her shoes match with silver glitter. Diane's smiling and waves to me as she clutches her Elmo doll.

"Mrs. Robbins, Because of the nature of this report, I need to see Diane's skin, even her buttocks, so I would appreciate it if you would remove her clothing for me."

"I can't believe somebody called. Who would do such a thing? I would never hurt my child. My husband and I don't smoke and the babysitter, Michelle doesn't either. I can't believe that this is happening. Ray should know about this."

"Mrs. Robbins, I know that this is very upsetting. How about if I take a look and if there are burns then we will need to speak with your husband? If not, I will leave my card and he can call me when he gets off of work. "

Mindy, places Diane on the living room carpet and takes off her T-shirt and then removes her pants including underwear. There are no marks on this child at all. I take a deep breath.

"Mrs. Robbins, all looks well. I don't know who contacted the State Hot Line as the caller was anonymous, so therefore I have no way of getting in touch with the individual that called. If your husband wants to talk with me, here is my professional card. I will not be visiting again regarding this report. Thank you for your cooperation." *Investigation closed...too easy.*

I give a big smile to Diane, and shake Mindy's hand. She gives a shy smile, and escorts us to the front door. The steps are knee deep in snow. Greg goes out first and waits to give me a hand. We walk towards the car, heads down, trying hard not to fall. The wind pushes us to the car. We fall into the car. The cold snow gets inside my right boot and I remove it, attempting to shake out the snow. Greg smiles as a sea gull cries overhead.

The weather continues to be menacing. Doug's following the horse trailer driven by Mike over to Elizabeth Allen's farm. Sammy clears a path over the bridge and waves goodbye to Mike and Doug. The bridge is dangerous. High winds are moving the stock trailer from side to side, coupled with the intensity of the blinding snow. Doug watches as Mike's trailer sways and weaves. His stomach is in knots. A cigarette would be a welcomed relief. To hell with taking that medicine; what with weird dreams and a libido like a teenager, Doug feels off balanced. He's anxious. This drive to the mainland is making Doug's knuckles white from fear not cold.

Mike's trailer sways and continues to weave. *Damn Mike, he's crazy. He needs to slow down!* Doug's stomach rumbles. Between the four foals showing up at the corral, trying to quit smoking and this weather, it's enough worry to make him lose it. God, he needs to hold it together. Not having a full time job is getting to him. Substitute teaching is getting to him. The kids are driving him crazy and Norma's stuck plucking chickens and carrying their medical insurance. Doug feels guilty, as he's supposed to be the breadwinner. He's old fashioned. Feeling guilty for financial difficulties, Doug's quit smoking and drinking. Money's tight. Doug considers himself a nice guy, however; without full-time employment and quitting smoking and drinking, he's ready to go off. For this moment, figuring out who's the asshole that left these foals to die and a cigarette would settle him. Doug clutches the steering wheel and pretends that he's inhaling and exhaling a Camel. *God, I need to start smoking again. I haven't felt right in four weeks. I have no money to smoke. How can I smoke when Norma can't get a pedicure? What a pisser.*

Doug continues following Mike, who's driving like it's a clear summer day. Doug barely makes out Wallops Island. A left at Wallops Island and they're almost to Elizabeth Allen's farm. Beth Keller's place is across the street just parallel to Elizabeth's place. Thinking of Beth, Doug feels a rush in his loins. *What a prize that young thing is. She took years off of me the other night at AJ's.*

Mike makes a wide left. The foals shift almost falling to the floor of the trailer. Doug continues to follow. Mike makes another left to Elizabeth Allen's farm. He drives up to the barn, parks and steps away from his truck. Russ gets out too. Elizabeth's Corgi, Princess runs from the barn to greet them. Only her head's showing from the depth of snow. Princess is excited as she's jumping up and down, scattering freshly fallen snow with every heartfelt spring. Famous for digging holes that every visitor has tripped-up and almost broke an ankle, Mike is glad that the snow is on the ground. Hopefully, with the depth of the snow nobody will trip and the foals will make it safely to the barn.

Elizabeth's standing at the opening of the barn with Beth as Doug arrives. He parks close to Mike and begins to walk to the barn.

"Beth and I were getting worried as to where you were. We have three nanny goats and one mare. Tiffany, my Arab, lost her foal to septicemia, a few weeks ago. She still has milk. Although she's high strung I think that once the foal starts to nurse she'll accept it. I have four stalls, two across the aisle from each other with fresh hay, water and shavings. The nanny goats that Beth brought over are in excellent condition and have good dispositions. We don't see a problem with the nanny's stalled with the foals. If need be I'll bottle feed goat milk. I think if we do have a problem it will be with Tiffany. I've given her a sedative so I'm hoping that she will be calm and permit the foal to nurse."

Mike and Russ walk to the backside of the trailer, open it and proceed into the stock trailer. Doug follows. Beth and Elizabeth stand on each side of the ramp, just in case a foal moves from the ramp. Russ, leads the first, Doug, the second and Mike the third. The fourth is too weak to walk, so Beth and Elizabeth stay with it until Russ returns. The weakest foal will be with Tiffany. Russ helps Beth and Elizabeth maneuver the foal to Tiffany's stall. Tiffany's excited. With the commotion in the barn and a sickly foal suddenly appearing in her stall; it's apparent that this situation is too much for the mare. Tiffany's eyes flare and she's prancing. Elizabeth and Beth introduce the foal to Tiffany who spins around and squeals. The foal's too weak to stand on her own. She falls over. Mike rushes into the stall and stands next to Russ. Russ is holding Tiffany by her halter. Mike grabs the lead and jerks it, pissing off Russ and Elizabeth. Russ shakes his head in disbelief. Elizabeth and Beth help the foal stand and walk the foal to Tiffany. The mare rears. Doug's watching and shakes his head too.

"Mike, I can tell that you have never read any articles by John Lyons, one of the most accomplished and respected horse practitioners in the world." Russ says as he takes the lead rope from Mike.

"Russ, why don't you hold Tiffany still and make her stand."

"Mike, I don't feel that it is necessary to traumatize my horse. I've tranquilized her. Let's calm down and wait for the tranquiller to take effect. Tiffany's feeling everybody's stress. I can always bottle feed the weak foal with goat milk. We've got plenty of milk."

Beth interjects, "I don't think that this is going to work right this second with Tiffany. Elizabeth's correct, let's just let things calm down and evaluate this situation. I do have a few more nannies and wouldn't mind loaning more. Anything I can do to help."

Beth and Elizabeth back out of the stall as does Russ and Mike. Doug has made himself comfortable watching from the aisle.

Doug clearing his throat gives Beth a wink and smile, "OK...let's just wait. Elizabeth's right. Let's all try to relax. We've got a major problem on our hands that we need to sort out."

Several minutes pass as everybody's looking into stalls. The goats and foals are accepting. Beth initially squirted goat milk at each of the foals. The foals latched and goats are standing and permitting the foals to nurse. It's Tiffany and the weak foal that are having difficulty.

Doug removes his cap and scratches his head, "I've never in my life seen anything like this. Where in the world did these foals come from? Who would leave foals out in these elements? We know one thing; these foals aren't descendents of Chincoteague ponies. Does anybody have a cigarette?"

"No, and you aren't starting to smoke Doug and you aren't smoking in my barn."

"Who put you in charge?"

"This is my land, my barn and you're not smoking. Over my dead body!"

"Changing the subject guys, I can't imagine where the mares are that gave birth to these young babies...and who would have put them in the pen." Beth says as she walks closer to the first stall to observe the nanny and foal, hoping to change the atmosphere within the barn.

Doug follows Beth and stands next to her. She can feel his eyes on her and his body heat.

Elizabeth and Russ look into Tiffany's stall. The weak foal has staggered to the mare and has latched onto her teat. Tiffany is standing still, her back legs apart and is permitting the foal to nurse.

Elizabeth takes a deep breath and looks up to the rafters of the barn, placing her hands together in a silent prayer.

"Now that Tiffany is tranquil how about if we leave the barn, and go back to the house as I've left a pot of coffee going, and have some freshly baked banana bread. This has been very stressful and we need to take a break and think about this situation."

Elizabeth turns and leaves the barn with Princess at her heals. She sees the depth of the snow and picks up her dog. "Sorry girl it's too deep for you."

Russ and Mike follow as Beth and Doug linger inside the barn.

"How about a quickie?"

"You can't be serious. You're either nuts or delusional. What happened the other evening was a onetime event. It just happened in a moment of drunkenness. Get over it. I'm friends with your wife; in fact I'm better friends with Norma than you. You and I aren't friends, lovers or soul mates. I regret what happened in the parking lot of AJ's. Move on."

Beth departs the barn in a huff, leaving Doug behind. She hears the words, "Bitch and whore" as she slides the barn door shut.

5

Beth Keller recently moved from Newark, New Jersey to the Eastern Shore. When she graduated from Newark High School, Beth had no skills, just good looks and a well-proportioned body. She found herself in the escort business. It was an avenue to earn quick cash. Forget working fast food; no money and long hours. And as for college, she had no desire.

Beth was smarter than most escorts, as she didn't get into drugs and saved her money. Her dream, a simple one, was to own a goat farm, and to produce feta cheese, just like her maternal great, grandparents in Greece. She located this sweet ranch with ten acres, already fenced, overlooking water and dunes, while surfing the Internet. The ranch was a foreclosure, and Beth didn't blink, she made a swift decision and with $5,000 down, it was hers.

Beth has fallen in love with life's tempo of the shore. Everybody's friendly. She's joined a local book club and has new friends, Norma, who's married to Doug Fields, an unemployed Salt Water Cowboy; Elizabeth Allen, her horsey neighbor and Francie Batista, who's a social worker and boards her horse at Elizabeth's farm.

Beth enjoys bartending at AJ's on the Creek, a popular island bar and restaurant located in Chincoteague. Beth craves the bar scene. As a bartender she spends the night flirting and smiling, and with great customer service skills, the tips are paying her mortgage. After escorting for five years, bartending is an avenue for quick money and easy work. Beth has learned to keep her drinking under control and is on guard as to whom she mingles with after hours. She enjoys meeting male tourists, especially the married ones. Men in their forties and fifties like a good time and have money to spend, especially the balding, and boxer underwear wearing pot-bellied ones.

JIGSAW Teresa Adele Bettino

The snow continues as I try to dry the inside of my right boot. Deputy Greg Franks turns up the heat and I use the car's heater to get the inside of my boot dry. The car pitches to the left and Greg puts his vehicle in 4-wheel drive.

"Greg, did you know that today is my birthday of all days."

"Happy Birthday, Francie. No I didn't know. Sorry. You sound so down. Do you have any plans?"

"My mom, who lives in Charlottesville, was coming today. I haven't heard from mom yet, but I know that she will cancel. There's too much snow for traveling."

"I'm sorry, Francie. Is there anything I can do to help you feel a little better?"

Um....I'm wondering where this conversation is going?

"You're right, Frank, I am down. Really I'm feeling frustrated and depressed. I miss not visiting with my mother and I'm miserable. I have four investigations to begin so I need to stay focused and worry about my mental health later this evening."

"I understand. I only travel home to Albuquerque twice a year to visit my family."

I'm ignoring this family talk. It's hitting too close to home. I'm suffering from mega emotional pain today.

"Greg, how about if we continue to my next child protective service report? I received this one today and it's on the island also. Do you know Frank and Margaret Adams? They have a sixteen- year-old daughter Ella. Ella's been thrown out of the house as Frank and Margaret don't like her boyfriend. Ella's staying with the next-door neighbor, Mary Landers. How about if I interview Ella first and parents second?"

"Alright. What's the street?"

"Let me see, it's on Deep Hole Road. Oh God, do you recall the last time that you and I worked a case on this street? To this day I still remember the smell of death."

"I know. I lost my lunch from Sugarbakers that day."

"I lost my Bill's flounder."

JIGSAW Teresa Adele Bettino

We both shake our heads and exhale. "How about if we change the subject and talk about a brighter subject. Greg, you're from New Mexico. Tell me what New Mexico's all about."

"I grew up in Albuquerque, which is a pretty large city. My parents are second generation Mexicans who work hard in a family owned Mexican restaurant. I attended the University of New Mexico majoring in criminal justice. I always knew that I didn't want to be a part of the restaurant business and didn't want to live in Albuquerque. Once I graduated, I went on-line and found a position through the Virginia Employment Commission for a job as a sheriff's deputy, so I applied and here I am. The hardest adjustment for me has been living around water. I almost lost it traveling the Chesapeake Bay Bridge Tunnel. I had never been over a bridge that long with tunnels to boot!"

"Definitely not good for anybody phobic."

We continue to inch our way towards the northeast section of the island. I notice that Greg has a frown line between his eyebrows. He's not bad looking with dark wavy hair and eyes almost black, kind-of rugged looking.

"Do you go home for visits often?"

"I return twice a year. By working this job, I get lots of over time so I fly home at Christmas and around Easter. I have a large family of cousins, aunts and uncles, so we hang out. I get my fill of Mexican food, return to Chincoteague and load up on fish." Greg laughs and moves the vehicle to the right, away from a drift.

"Your name Franks doesn't sound Mexican. I'm sorry I shouldn't have said that as I'm stereotyping."

"No it's OK. My grandparents' last name is Franco. When they came to New Mexico they changed it to Franks. They wanted to be American. It's similar to immigrants in the early 1900's coming over from Italy, Spain, Germany."

The guys intelligent.

"You're right. As you probably are aware, I am Italian. My great- great grandparents came over from Rome. They kept their names and opened a pizza restaurant in Little Italy, New York."

Greg makes a left and we're on Deep Hole Road, one of the oldest areas of the island. As we arrive and park in front of Mary Lander's white-framed house, I see the curtain move.

"Well Greg, this is good. I just saw the curtain move." I quickly put my mucking boot on and Greg turns off the cruiser. I get out. The snow's just below my knees.

"Greg, I can't believe how deep this is. Maybe the governor will declare a State of Emergency?"

"I hope not. I'll have to pull twelve hour shifts."

I can barely climb the front steps so Greg helps. We slip our way to the door and I manage to knock prior to almost falling from the porch. Greg grabs my arm to steady me.

The door opens and I show my social service ID, "I'm Francie Batista and am looking for Mary Landers and Ella Adams. Are you Mary Landers?"

"Yes, what exactly do you want missy?"

"Social services received a child protective report about Ella not living at home because of her boyfriend. It is my understanding that you have taken her in. I need to discuss this situation with you and also with Ella. Also, Deputy Franks is with me due to the weather as I can't drive the county car."

Ms. Landers permits access to her dark living room.

"Well, I don't have anything to say about Margaret and Frank kicking their daughter out of the house. You can speak with Ella. I'm not talking to nobody. She's in the guest bedroom down the hallway to the right."

"I don't feel comfortable going down the hallway and speaking with Ella in her bedroom. I would prefer that she comes into the living room and that I interview her alone."

"Whatever," and out of the living room Mary strolls.

I glance over to Greg, who rolls his eyes and glances around the room. *Yes, I know it is really dark in this room especially with the painted black walls.* He obviously isn't going to take a seat on the sofa.

Mary returns with a disheveled looking Ella Adams, who's wearing an oversized wool sweater and holey jeans. Her long red hair is in a pony tail and she's barefooted. Obviously she's been sleeping off stress and nasty weather."

"Hi, Ella. I'm Francie Batista, a local social worker and I need to speak with you for a few minutes." I shoot Mary a look and she turns leaving the living room and entering her kitchen. I can hear her walking about the kitchen, clanging a pot. I know that she's going to be eavesdropping by her actions.

"What do you want?"

"I want to speak with you about why you aren't living with your parents. Somebody who is concerned about your situation called social services and wanted a social worker to speak with you and your mom and dad."

"Oh, whatever."

"The report says that there is conflict between your parents and you and the fact that you are dating this guy named...let me see Romeo, maybe I have his name wrong."

"No you got it right. He's from Newport News and his name is Romeo Ramirez. I met him at our high school football game."

"So what's going on with your parents about him?"

"Well, I snuck him in the house into my bedroom, which is upstairs. My parents' room is downstairs under mine. We were getting it on, when his foot hit the closet door, and the door fell off its hinge and hit the floor. The noise woke Mom and Dad. Dad came into the room to investigate and caught us fucking. *I look over to Greg whose smiling.* Dad started yelling to Mom to get the shotgun; Romeo freaked, ran out of the house without his pants, underwear, socks, shoes and his winter coat. Dad's grounded me for life. So, I walked. Right out the front door and came over here. Mary's a friend of mine and says that I can stay forever. To hell with my parents."

"Well, one problem is that you are sixteen and not eighteen and you are considered a minor. It's your parents' responsibility to provide, food, clothing and shelter until you're eighteen."

"So...your point..."

"Excuse me, Ms. Batista. Ella, you didn't tell me that you and Romeo were fornicating. That is a totally different story then what you told me."

Ella is looking a little embarrassed. Her face is matching her hair and her foot is starting to shake back and forth as she sits in the living room rocker moving back and forth at an alarming rate.

Mary takes a seat next to me on the sofa. She turns on a brighter light. "Ella, you told me that you were kicked out of the house as you had gotten an F in Spanish."

Ella looks down at her shaking foot. She's in need of a major pedicure. Chipped nails and calluses along with a hammertoe. *I bet her foot hurts when she wears heels.*

"Ms. Batista, can I speak with you alone?"

Ella leaves in a flash and Mary moves to the rocker. *God I hope she doesn't get too comfortable....snow is going to be up to my ass by the time we leave here at this rate. I catch Greg giving me a look as he moves to look out the living room window. He moves the curtain and gasps; totally, not good.*

"After hearing that she was having sex before marriage, I don't want her in my house. What a hussy."

"Well, Mary...Ms. Landers, you will explain this to Ella as Ella and her parents need to straighten this out. I can help with some family counseling. I wouldn't think too harshly about Ella. You liked her before you knew that she was having sex, and I really feel that she considers you as her friend. So, spend a few minutes explaining to Ella."

Mary gets up and walks down the hallway returning with Ella. Greg continues standing, at times shifting his weight. He has the patience of a saint.

"Ella, Mary has something to say to you. I am here to listen and to help you. My goal is to work through this situation with your parents and you." *God working with teenagers is crippling. I need some wine and a joint. I need to relax. My neck is getting stiff and I need some chocolate.*

"Well, Ms. Batista. You can do what you want. I'm not going home and you can kiss my ass."

"You will need to show respect for Ms. Batista, or else I will be throwing you in a detention center for a couple of week's snow or no snow, Christmas or no Christmas." *Greg's taking a dominate role...good going.*

Ella turns and leaves the living room. "I want her out of my house. This is what the county pays you for Ms. Batista and I want her out of here right now!"

"Mary, you need to calm down. Prior to my coming, you were harboring Ella and didn't think twice. Now that you have heard what transpired you are throwing this situation into my lap. Yes, I am paid by the county. We are in the middle of a snowstorm and unless Ella agrees to return home, she will need to stay here until other arrangements can be made. I don't have any foster homes that will take a teenager on such short notice, especially today. What I plan to do is to go over to Mr. and Mrs. Adams home and speak with them about this situation. A plan will need to be formulated. I will get back with you. Next time, don't be so eager to take in a teenager, as you have helped to enable Ella not to return home. This is a mess and you have helped to make it a big one."

I swiftly get up from the couch and open the front door. I can't see the path that Greg and I made coming into this home. Greg follows as I creep down the steps holding sternly to the railing. *Happy Birthday to me, what bullshit.* I walk across the yard to the Adams residence. I am pissed. I hate it when these godly people get involved with saving a teenager and then the situation turns sour. Mary was fine until she realized that Ella wasn't the Virgin Mary.

I walk up a mound of snow to the front porch and briskly knock. Frank Adams answers the door. He opens it wide and appears nervous. Greg appears behind me and I quickly introduce myself, show my ID and explain my presence. Greg introduces himself and I explain that he's driving me around due to the weather. Frank still appears nervous as he opens the screen door to let us in. The moment I enter, I smell a faint scent of cannabis sativa. I smile and inhale. Greg doesn't appear to smell anything.

Margaret enters the living room, which is very colorful with a mixture of antiques and contemporary, very eclectic. It's bright and shows much life, unlike Mary's home. There's a bouquet of white roses in the corner of the room with a photo of Mary, Frank and Ella during happier days.

"Hi, Mrs. Adams. I'm Francie Batista, a social worker and I am here to speak with you about what happened a couple of days ago which caused Ella to leave and somebody to contact the department of social services to request a home visit. So, if you or Mr. Adams could explain, I'd appreciate it. I have visited next-door and have briefly spoken to Ella and Mary Landers."

"Well, I was sleeping at the time that this happened so I will let my husband talk."

"You see, as my wife was saying she was asleep at the time and I was awakened by some loud crash. I went upstairs to check on Ella and when I opened her bedroom door, she was on the floor with her boyfriend Romeo. I didn't even know that she had a boyfriend. They were both nude and you know what they were doing. I don't need to say it."

"OK. *I can guess what direction this is headed.* So what happened?"

"I became outraged that my daughter first of all would be doing this at age sixteen, secondly that she would have the audacity to have sex in my house, under my roof, while my wife and I were sleeping down stairs and third of all, that this brazen boy would come into my home and screw my daughter." *Frank needs some more pot. He's going to have a massive heart attack.*

"Alright. I do understand your level of anger, as well as; concern for the wellbeing of your daughter. So what happened after you came upon this scene."

"Well, um…Ms. Batista, can I call you Francie? *Oh Lordy-Lord, this is going to be an entire day affair with Margaret telling the story. Maybe Frank does need to have a massive heart attack so that we can cut to the chase.*

"Of course you can call me Francie and if it's fine with you, I will refer to you as Margaret."

"That's okay. Anyway, Frank started screaming, Ella started screaming and Romeo flew down the steps nude out into the winter air. I ran upstairs and saw Ella wrapped in a quilt and the closet door on the floor. Frank was livid. I have never seen him so angry. He told Ella that this was against the house rules. She said that she was going to do what the hell she pleased. Frank told her to leave and then Frank walked out of Ella's bedroom. I stayed and asked Ella what happened. She told me that she was having sex with her boyfriend, Romeo. I didn't even know that she was dating anybody. She said that she was in love with him, wanted to marry him and would do what she wanted. Ella then got up from her bed, and threw on some jeans, a sweater, and flip-flops. She gathered her laptop, cell phone and purse and out the door she went."

I look over to see Greg, as he's shifting his weight to his left leg. His eyes show somebody whose finding this scene humorous as his dark eyes are smiling. "So, what do you want to do about this situation? Your daughter can't continue to stay with Mary Landers. Ms. Landers wants Ella out. Your daughter told her an entirely different story and now that Mary understands that Ella was having intercourse, she wants her gone."

Frank begins to tear up. Margaret takes his hand and gently pats it. "I want Ella to come home. I think that we need counseling. Ella needs to follow household rules. Ella is our only child. *Thank God for me.* I want my child to come home." Margaret lets out one very large sob as Frank folds into his wife's opened arms. He's bawling right along with her. *Saint Anthony of hopeless causes and lost things, I will pray to you every night! This is definitely going to have a happy ending.*

"Well, if it is all right with you, I will walk next-door and speak with your daughter. She will be coming home. I have some names of family counselors in the area so that you can connect with one of them and commence family work."

I turn and look over at Greg. He gives me a nod. I open the front door and am blasted by wind and snow. As I make my way slowly down the front steps, the snow's high enough that it enters both mucking boots, drips down to the top of my foot making my bones ache. I slip a few times, make it to Mary Lander's porch, and miraculously the front door opens. Mary's excited, as she wants me to fix things fast. I can tell that she's spoken with Ella as Ella's holding her lap top, cell phone and pocketbook. She looks as though she's been crying.

"Ella, it looks to me that you're ready to return home. Your parents want you to come home and are prepared to begin family counseling. They love you very much. You are their only child. They want what's best for you." *Boy it's amazing how good I am at bullshitting and I've only worked for the welfare department for a few years. Just think how good I'll be by the time I retire, that's if I make it that long.*

Like Margaret, Ella burst into tears and leaves Mary's home following me across the yard. Ella isn't wearing boots, only flip-flops and she begins to crow-hop quickly home, passing me. We arrive; Ella to the open arms of both parents and me dreading this day and wanting to vacate. I'll check-up on the Adams family in a few days.

"Greg, I really need to get back to the agency to see how things are going. Chip's been by himself for a while. I will need someone from your department to transport me tomorrow as I have two adult protective service reports to go out on, both of which are on the mainland."

"We have a mandatory meeting late in the afternoon so if you want me to pick you up around nine, we'll be able to go out on those reports. The meeting tomorrow is to announce our new captain."

Greg parks in front of the agency. I can see that Jon's been busy clearing the sidewalk down Main Street so it's easy for me to walk to enter the waiting room without getting any more snow inside of my mucking boots or falling. Nobody's waiting, which is quite unusual. Chip Wells is sitting with his back to the waiting area looking at the snowy park. Bella and Sergeant run from my back office to greet me. They're quite excited, and a little damp. Chip must have had the dogs out playing in the park.

"Hey Chip, how's it going?"

"OK. I'm tired and hungry. Francie, I'm taking a break. Finally, the waiting room is vacant."

"Yep. Snow has a way of parting the sea around here."

"Do you think you can stay and answer phones? I'd love to run over to Bill's and have a well nourished lunch."

"No problem. Take as long as you want. I have lots of computer work to complete and I need to make a few calls."

Chip puts on his western wear and leaves. I quickly call Kaylee and inform her where Chip's eating lunch. Within two minutes, as I look out the front window, I see Kaylee leaving the mall headed for Bill's. I return to my office with the dogs trailing behind.

The snow continues in force with howling winds whistling. I need to call Elizabeth Allen to see how my horse, Trooper's doing. There's no way I can travel to the mainland driving my Honda Civic or the county Chevrolet to visit him. As I pick up the phone to call Elizabeth, another chill runs up and down my spine. I put the phone down, turn around and look outside my window. Sleet begins to pelt on the roof and windows. I'm thinking of my mother, she hasn't called and the day's ominous.

6

Gertrude Batista covers her head, not wanting to see all the snow, especially on her daughter's twenty-fifth birthday. Like her daughter, Gertrude hates the snow, hates winter and hates the sunless skies that Virginia frequently offers during the dreary months of December, January and February.

She's pushed herself out of bed earlier to feed her two horses and to check on the barn yard cats, which were cozily sleeping this winter's day wrapped together laying between bales of hay. Gertrude's horses, Bronco and Jester, Quarter horse geldings welcomed their morning mash; warm water mixed carrots, sliced apples with grain. Prior to leaving them happily eating their morning meal Gertrude gave them two flakes of hay and checked their water. With the heaters working and everybody contented, Gertrude trudged back to the house.

In the company of her dog, Buddy, a hound mix, who bounded merrily by her side, Gertrude sighed heavily and once inside the warmth of her kitchen, she made a hot cup of tea adding honey and lemon and decided to go back to bed. Retired, for one year, she relishes not having to go outside in the elements and drive to work. Gertrude's first retirement year has had major change. Relocating from Richmond and moving to a small farm, just outside the town of Charlottesville has been an adjustment. Getting away from humans and taking care of animals is just what the doctor ordered.

Gertrude had planned to visit Francie today. Drive to Chincoteague, treat her only child to dinner and spend a few days shopping and enjoying the shore. She had arranged for her friend and fix-it man, Lonnie to watch the farm and was looking forward to getting away for a few days. Gertrude has worried about Francie this past year. Emotionally, Francie has not fully recovered from almost getting murdered, seeing two dead clients and her horse almost getting shot in the head by Bart Connors. On the brighter side, the incarceration of Francie's supervisor Sally-Sue Moon, for possession of pot, was a blessing, as Sally-

Sue was emotionally abusive to Francie. Thank God for Francie's friend Jodi Burgess, who has called Gertrude weekly reporting on her daughter's wellbeing.

Gertrude sighs again and looks out the window seeing gray and white. The snow's coming up from the south, and it's going to be a crippler. Virginia doesn't do well with snow. Secondary streets don't get plowed and schools are out for weeks at a time. She takes another sip of her Earl Gray tea continuing to look at snow and gray. She notices that a vehicle is making its way slowly up her graveled road. As it arrives, Gertrude notices that it's a taxicab covered with ice and snow and it has stopped in front of her house. Gertrude leaves her tea on the kitchen table and walks to the front door with Buddy at her heels. As she opens the door, snow flies into her foyer. The cab's lettering indicates that it is from Charlottesville. Gertrude's confused. Who could be visiting?

The cab driver, a young man, springs from the driver's side and quickly opens the driver's side back door. A frail elderly lady is helped from the back seat clutching her leather pocketbook. She is unkempt looking in dress and style and stares at the house and Gertrude. The cabby opens the trunk and carries a crumbled looking suitcase up the snowy steps to the front door. He returns to his vehicle and helps this frail woman walk through ever mounting snow. She climbs the front steps, without a smile and stares.

"Excuse me sir, what's going on?"

"This lady here came up from Louisiana by bus, got off in Richmond, got on another bus to Charlottesville and gave me this address. I didn't even know that this address existed in the Charlottesville area. I haven't been this far out before."

"What! I don't know her."

The woman makes her way into the foyer and bends to pet Buddy, who's wagging his tail.

"Sir, you can't be serious."

"I'm as serious as a heart attack and want to get the hell out of here before I get stuck. The fare's a hundred bucks!"

"There's no way that you expect me to pay. I don't know this woman. She needs to go back to town with you. You can call the police when you get there."

"Hell no. I'm leaving."

The cab driver walks over to the mysterious disheveled woman with his hand out. "Ma'am I want a hundred bucks."

She opens her old purse, an alligator bag with an unaltered vacant alligator face attached. Empty eyes stare surrounded by crinkled leather as this lady hands the cabby a one hundred dollar bill. With wrinkled hands, she gives the cab driver his money and quickly snaps her purse shut. This unknown woman proceeds to walk into the living room. Once inside the living room, she picks up family pictures from a table, studies the photos and proceeds to sit in an old rocking chair. She begins to rock. Buddy lies next to her.

Energized the cabby makes an about-face and hightails it out of the house down icy snowy steps. He sprints to his cab, leaping onto the driver's seat. Within one minute he's seen sliding down the drifting driveway leading to the country road heading for Charlottesville.

This can't be happening. I must be dreaming. I just saw my doctor about hot flashes, night sweats and forgetfulness. I just started taking Premarin last week to help me get through menopause. Maybe this is a side effect?

The lady stops rocking. "Where's my son, Rick?"

"Ma'am, I am the only person residing here. There is no Rick here."

"What have you done with my son?"

Oh God, this isn't the medicine. It would be great if this were a scene from "Saturday Night Live" but it isn't. This woman is demented or psychotic. Take your pick.

"Excuse me, but the cab driver said that you were from Louisiana and that you took a bus from Louisiana, got off in Richmond, got back on another bus and came to Charlottesville. What's the reason Ma'am that you're traveling in this weather?"

"My son, Rick lives here. I left my husband, Pierre. He's a cheating bastard. I went into my closet and another woman's clothes are there. I got on the next bus leaving New Orleans. I want to divorce my husband and live with my son."

Gertrude takes a deep breath, just like she did over one year ago when working with the aged.

"Ma'am why don't we go into the kitchen and I will make you a cup of tea and cook you something to eat? By the way, if you could tell me your name that would be wonderful."

"My name is Marie Theresa LaSlick and I want to see my son." Marie Theresa demands as she abruptly launches herself from the rocking chair. Gertrude turns and begins walking to the kitchen with Mrs. LaSlick and Buddy following, his tail wagging with much eagerness.

Gertrude quickly boils some water for tea, and makes scrambled eggs and toast adding jam for sweetness. It's apparent that Mrs. LaSlick hasn't eaten for a while as she devours the eggs and toast. The tea cup, she holds as a lady, with pinky out and uses her napkin delicately.

"Mrs. LaSlick do you have any phone numbers of family members in your pocketbook or suitcase?

"Yes, I have Rick's number."

"Can I call him so I can let him know that you're with me?"

"That would be fine. If you can get my purse, I will give you the number."

As Gertrude leaves the kitchen and enters the living room, she looks outside. High drifts have formed and the gravel driveway is invisible. She picks up Mrs. LaSlick's pocketbook from the floor, looks at the alligator's face and shakes her head. The eyes stare back. Gertrude shudders.

Gertrude returns to the kitchen, as Mrs. LaSlick falls from the kitchen chair landing on the linoleum floor with a large thud. Gertrude, drops the purse, and is helping her uninvited guest up from the floor when there's a cracking noise from the nearby woods, a transformer perhaps, as the electricity blinks off, on and off. *This can't be happening to me. I'm in a deep sweat, hot flashing every second, screw the Premarin, I need a drink to calm my nerves.*

Elizabeth, Doug, Mike, Russ and Beth are sitting in Elizabeth's kitchen having coffee, hot tea and freshly baked goodies when the phone rings. It's Francie Batista and she wants to know how Trooper is and generally how Elizabeth's managing. Everybody at the table shakes their heads.

"How's life in all of this snow, Elizabeth?" Francie questions as she watches a cat trying to walk on the snowy dock.

"You won't believe this Francie, but four foals were found at the Corral Pen in Assateague and they're at my farm. Goats from Beth's farm and my horse, Tiffany are nursing them as we speak. They are very weak. We're trying to figure out who left them there and where their dams are."

"I don't believe this. How could anybody do anything like that? Have you contacted the sheriff's department and the animal warden for neglect?"

"We haven't gotten to that point Francie. We're sitting here having coffee and tea as we've just returned from the barn. Oh, while I have you on the phone, Russ wanted to talk to you."

Francie grabs goodies from her desk bottom right drawer. Chocolate kisses with a combination of potato chips will do.

"Hi, Russ, is there something wrong with Trooper?"

"No, I just wanted to let you know that he threw a shoe again. His back left. I don't have my stuff with me. Do you want me to come back tomorrow and re-shoe?"

"If you can make it back there that would be good. Why do you think he keeps throwing his back left shoe?"

"Trooper is slightly off. It's no big deal and nothing to be concerned about Francie. I'm going to have my friend, a chiropractor adjust him. We'll work on keeping him balanced that way he won't be stiff on one side and won't throw a shoe."

"OK. Thanks so much Russ. Can you put Elizabeth back on?"

"Elizabeth, I wish that I could help you, but right now there's no way that I can get off this island. I'm happy that you and Beth are able to help these foals."

Elizabeth and Francie hang up. Elizabeth smiles and returns to the kitchen table.

"Francie suggested that we call the sheriff's department and register a complaint with the animal warden. Who's our warden these days?"

"Our warden's Warren McKinney. I can call him if you want?" Doug says as he reaches for a second helping of carbs. By not smoking and getting healthy he's gaining weight and will probably die from a heart attack instead of lung cancer.

"I think that's our next step." Beth says getting up from the table and walking to the back window, near the counter where the coffee pot is. "Do you want a refill, Elizabeth?"

"No." Elizabeth pushes the kitchen antique oak chair back and joins Beth looking outside. As she stares she can't believe that the barn isn't visible. "This snow, I don't believe this storm. It's very unusual for Virginia." She walks over to Doug, shoves a piece of bread into her mouth, cuts a slice of banana bread, smears cream cheese on it and takes her seat at the kitchen table.

"If I continue to eat at this rate, by spring I won't be recognizable."

Doug laughs drinks some coffee loaded with sugar, pulls his cell phone from his right jean pocket and proceeds to call the sheriff's department. Brittany, retired Chief Winston's breath of sunshine answers the phone.

"Hi Brittany this is Doug Fields. We have a situation that needs to be reported to the sheriff's department and also to the animal warden, Warren McKinney.''

"OK. Due to the weather, I'll take the report over the phone."

As Doug proceeds to explain, Elizabeth, Mike and Russ decide to walk to the barn. Elizabeth places a winter coat on Princess and they bound to the barn. Beth loses sight of them in a second. She can't get over this weather too. New Jersey has its fair share of poor weather, however; living in Newark and in the city is a lot different than living on a goat farm in what feels like the wilderness. Beth shakes at the thought of losing electricity, heat and water. *What if the goats get sick and if the water trough freezes? I'm not prepared for this and how am I going to get to work. I need money to pay the mortgage. This is freaking me out.*

Doug ends his conversation with Brittany and helps himself to another cup of coffee. He sees concern on Beth's face.

"Beth, you look upset."

"I'm freaking out about this weather. Although I'm from New Jersey, I've not lived in a rural area and am concerned about the welfare of my goats in the event that the electricity goes off."

"You don't have a generator?"

"No, I hadn't even thought of getting one."

"Well, if push comes to shove, I'm sure that Elizabeth would help you with your goats. She has a generator and some extra stalls. You really don't need to worry."

Beth smiles and resumes looking outside. Elizabeth, Mike, Russ and Princess have probably entered the barn by now. The sound of the kitchen door opening, returns Beth to the moment. Mike has returned, he's blowing his warm breath over his hands and is covered with a layer of snow. Beth hadn't seen him walking back with the degree of snow falling. He stands by the door, knocking snow from his body and carefully removes his boots.

"The foals have settled and are looking a lot better. Doug I really need to be getting back. Can you give Russ a ride? He's about to look at Trooper's hooves. The horse has such a history of throwing shoes, he's thinking of just trimming and letting each hoof grow out."

"No problem. I need to give Norma a call to see if she needs anything from the food store while I'm out and about. I want to let her know that I've made it to Elizabeth's farm." Doug shifts his eyes to Beth, who rolls hers. Beth continues sitting at the table clutching her mug of coffee. It appears to be her security blanket for the moment. The coffee has got to be cold by now.

Mike pours some hot tea into his cup and adds some local honey and lemon, taking a seat next to Beth. He sips it, eyeing Doug and Beth, then downs the rest and stands abruptly. He faces Beth and Doug, salutes and turns walking from the kitchen. In the distance Beth and Doug hear the engine crank.

"I wonder what he was smiling about."

"I really don't care one way or another. You need to call your wife; you do recall that you have one."

Doug walks away headed to the living room holding his cell phone in the palm of his hand. He walks to the picture window and stares at the blinding snow. He speed dials Norma.

"Hi honey it's me. Listen, I'm at Elizabeth's and we got the foals here at her farm. I've made a police report and am waiting to hear from the animal warden. I'm glad that you made it home safely. Do you need me to stop at the store for anything? I will be home in a few hours as I have to drop Russ off on my way back. This here is a bad one. Stay at home Norma."

"Doug, we do need some cat litter, milk and bread. Also some eggs."

"OK...if I can make it to the store without risking my life I will get you what we need. We do have pop corn as I like to watch movies."

"Doug, since you quit smoking, we have purchased all of the popping corn in Chincoteague."

"Just making sure. I'll see you in a few hours Norma. I love you."

Doug flicks the cell and returns to the kitchen. Beth hasn't moved. She's sitting at the kitchen table drinking coffee looking pathetic.

The front door opens and Princess enters with Elizabeth and Russ. Elizabeth removes Princess's coat and Princess gives a good shake and rolls. Elizabeth leans down gives Princess a pet and smiles knowing that Princess is going to travel to the wood stove, circle three times and lay down. She and Russ remove their coats and boots and walk in their stocking feet into the kitchen. They eye the bread, banana cake and coffee cake. The pot of hot coffee's still available.

"Everything's tight at the barn. What time are you planning to return to Chincoteague Doug?"

"In a few minutes. I was hanging out waiting for a call from Warren. I don't want to be trying to talk to him and driving. If he calls you Russ, you can explain what's up. How about if we leave? This is really getting bad. I'm scared the 4-wheel drive won't work."

Russ takes a last swig of his cold coffee, moves to the foyer putting his coat and boots on. Doug gets up, strolls across the kitchen, and places his coffee cup in the sink. He winks at Elizabeth, thanking her for her hospitality. As he walks along the kitchen table, he gently touches Beth's hair. Beth leans away as Doug joins Russ in the foyer. Beth and Elizabeth hear the front door close.

As the truck cautiously makes it way down the covered road, Elizabeth looks at Beth and groans. "This is a real mess we got here. Whose foals are they and why did somebody drop them at Assateague?"

"Do you know anybody that had any pregnant mares this late in the season?"

"No." Elizabeth says as she takes a bite from a sliver of coffee cake she has cut.

"Me either." I think we need to start our own investigation. "I wonder who has purchased land around here recently besides me."

Instead of snow landing on the roof, the sound of hail banging causes Princess to come into the kitchen and sit next to Elizabeth. Elizabeth's deep in thought wondering if she has enough gasoline for her generator. Beth gets up from the table, grabs her coat and places her hand on Elizabeth's shoulder.

"Elizabeth, this is my first winter in Virginia. I am freaking...please keep in touch with me. If my electricity goes off can I come over as I don't want to be alone?"

"Of course. Don't worry. Everything will be fine."

As Beth leaves through the kitchen door, Elizabeth realizes that she isn't prepared for this weather. Sea winds have combined with this storm from the south.

Beth begins her trek home. Hail hits her head, face and mouth. She stumbles and lands on icy snow. She picks herself up, and continues home. *Dear God and I thought New Jersey had bad winters.*

Mike Griffin turns onto Route 13 and is heading to Temperanceville. He's pissed and needs to deal with the asshole that dropped the foals off at the Corral Pen. Mike's been overseeing this operation and has been pocketing about five-hundred a week. He isn't about to lose this extra income because some asshole didn't do his job. Brittany loves jewelry, the latest fashions and money. He's got to get this problem fixed now...after all he's a Salt Water Cowboy.

7

Park Ranger Molly Smith's sitting at a booth at the Village Restaurant having a bowl of beef stew and coffee when she notices animal control officer Warren McKinney, sitting in the booth next to hers. She's recently met Warren at a Christmas party at the library. Molly picks up her bowl and mug and proceeds to invite herself to join Warren.

Warren began his position as animal control officer in November and doesn't know many islanders. He previously worked in Richmond for the SPCA. One afternoon he was surfing the Virginia Employment Commission's site and read that Chincoteague was in need of an animal control officer. Warren had experience as a school police officer so it was a perfect fit. An honor graduate from Virginia Commonwealth University, Warren received his criminal justice degree ten years ago.

"May I?"

"Please join me Molly. I didn't realize that you were here. I'm taking a break. This weather is too much."

"Have you heard what happened on Assateague?"

Just as Molly says Assateague Warren's cell phone and pager go off simultaneously.

"Um...this must be quite an emergency to get two pages at the same time."

"Believe me, if this is what I think it is, you bet."

"Excuse me Molly; I just want to take this outside in my jeep. I'll be right back."

Warren opens the restaurant's door, braces for the weather jogging to his jeep, hops in and returns Brittany's calls.

"Hi, Britt; Hey what's up."

"Warren, you need to call Doug Fields. In case you don't know who he is; he's a Salt Water Cowboy with a mess on his hands. In a few minutes you're going to be given this mess. Here's his number."

"Well, what the heck's going on Brittany?"

"Just give him a call and he'll tell you. I have to go. "

"Hey, wait a minute…what's the rush?"

Warren uses his cell and opens the window of his jeep. He doesn't give a hoot that the snow's coming inside. He feels like he's overheating. Doug's phone rings and goes to voice. He decides to chill…deep breathing. He attempts again and there's no pick up. Warren rolls up his window and jogs back inside the restaurant. Molly's finished eating and is having desert, peach cobbler with vanilla ice cream.

"So what's up, Warren?"

"I received a call from Brittany, the administrative assistant for the captain, and she directed me to call Doug Fields. Do you know him and what's this about as he didn't pick up his phone?"

"This morning when I was making rounds over in Assateague, I walked over to the Pony Corral and in the pen were four foals half dead."

"You can't be serious. Who the hell would do such a thing? Where are they now?"

"I'm serious…don't know who the hell did it…and they're at Elizabeth Allen's horse farm."

"Who's she?"

"I only know a little of the story so I will tell you what I know. Last year, she found a dead horse in her field. It was her friend's horse and the horse had been shot in the head and attached to the horse's hoof was a horse wind chime. It turns out that Bart Connors, now known as The Eastern Shore Wind Chime Killer, had killed the wrong horse. He was nuts and hated social workers. He later followed Francie Batista, the only social worker in Chincoteague and her friend, Investigator Jodi Burgess, to Key West, Florida, where he kidnapped Francie and attempted to kill her."

"My God! It sounds as though there was a lot going on with a killer loose on Chincoteague Island last year…and I thought this job was going to be low-key."

"I've only heard pieces of the story… as I'm new here too…there's more to it."

"Well, since I can't get in touch with Doug Fields, I'll contact Elizabeth Allen. Do you have her cell number?"

"No, but I can tell you how to get to her farm."

"Go over the bridge to Wallops, make a left and drive a little ways. You will see a sign Watts Estates on your left. Drive down the dirt road and her farm's the last on the left."

"Thanks a lot. Molly. Um… I've been meaning to ask you something. Would you like to go out to dinner one night?"

Molly's taken by surprise, smiles and pats her lip with her napkin. "That would be great. You have my cell number right?"

"Yeah, it's on an emergency sheet given to me last week at a meeting. I have it stashed at home. How about if I call you later tonight? I'm sure that due to this blizzard we will be at home reading a good novel and having a glass of wine. At least I know I will. I'll give you a call and maybe we can talk for awhile and plan a date for the near future."

"Yes, that sounds good." Molly says with a large smile. She can hardly contain herself as she hasn't had a date in awhile.

Warren excuses himself from the table and puts on his wet coat, gloves and hat. He's out the door in a flash. Molly continues eating the rest of her cobbler and ice cream thinking of her upcoming date. Warren seems nice enough, handsome with sandy colored hair, blue eyes, a nice smile and potentially a warm heart. He has a good build, probably spends time lifting weights at local a gym.

Molly calls her boss, Michael Reed.

"Mike, this is Molly. How are you?"

"We're getting hammered with a mixture of snow and ice. The governor's just declared a State of Emergency."

"I figured that the governor was going to do something. It's a mess on Chincoteague Island. I'm calling to inform you of an event that is probably going to make the newspapers."

"What could have happened on Assateague?"

"Somebody left four foals abandoned in the Corral Pen and I found them earlier today half frozen."

"You can't be serious...who would do something like that...and what's happened to the foals?"

"Well, I contacted Doug Fields, the contact for the Salt Water Cowboys, who organized some islanders to remove them. The foals are at a local horse farm on the mainland near Wallops."

"Did you notify the police and the animal warden?"

"Yes. I have just spoken with Warren, and he's on his way to Elizabeth Allen's farm where the foals have been placed. The police have been notified and are commencing an investigation."

"Molly, just continue what you're doing with patrolling the park. You have done everything according to policy. Good work and keep me posted."

"Before you hang up Mike, can I take the rest of the day off as I'm really stressed and need a break?"

"That's no problem. State offices are closed and we follow State guidelines when the governor declares an emergency."

"Thanks a bunch, Mike and I will keep you up to date regarding the abandoned foals."

Molly leaves the Villager, and is excited about not having to return to work. She desires to return home, put on her bathrobe, open a bottle of wine and continue reading James Patterson's book, *Double Cross*. Although the plot is set in New York, where a maniac is killing folks and leaving them in public areas, it could easily have occurred on Chincoteague. With a glass of wine and some chips, this will be a good day to get into bed, read, drink and eat. What else could she want? Well, maybe sex if Warren and she become an item.

Molly drives slowly. She's stressed driving in this weather and is having difficulty seeing Maddox Road...total whiteout. She keeps her truck in others faint tire tracks. As she reaches her driveway, she notices that a letter has been tacked to her front door. Molly's perplexed and quickly exits her truck, walking with purpose up her icy snowy steps. She pulls the note from the door. It's a hand written message, like a poem. Some of the ink has run down the page and now that she's reading this message in the elements, more ink is spreading down the page. Molly reads the note as she's unlocking her front door. Once inside her place she speed dials Warren.

It's about three in the afternoon and I'm sitting at my desk, not doing paperwork, just sitting and staring out the back window. I'm as depressed as I can get as the snow isn't stopping, mom hasn't called, and I'm feeling sorry for myself. I'm thinking about the four foals and wondering what the hell's going on. Who would do such a thing? Foals normally aren't born in the month of December, so I'm pretty perplexed. I'm deep in thought and hear the front door bell jangle. *Shit whose coming into the agency?*

I scoot my chair back, running over cases on the floor for about the tenth time today and spring from my chair. Sergeant follows. Bella's snoring and in a deep dream as her feet are moving a mile a minute and she is yelping softly as I walk from my office.

"Hey, partner in crime!"

"Hi, Jodi…what's up…twice in one day?"

"Oh nothing. I thought that I would check on you prior to going home. I know how you get in the winter and to top it off it's your birthday."

"I know. Mom hasn't called and I tried to call her. I'm starting to panic that she hasn't called. She was supposed to be coming down to visit me. Maybe she's stuck somewhere? Or something has happened to her. You know Jodi that it's not like her."

"I don't officially start work until Monday, let me give Charlottesville Sheriff's Department a call and ask a deputy to go check on your mom." OK girlfriend?

"Thanks Jodi. That makes me feel a lot better."

The front door jingles again, and since we're sitting in the reception area, we see Chip returning from lunch and waving good-bye to Kaylee as he shuts the agency door. He's covered in snow and some ice.

"Chip, you can go home if you want to. The governor has declared a State of Emergency and state offices are closed. This county office is closed too, as our supervisor, Paul, just called and informed me. I was just about to leave when Jodi came by."

"Say no more...I'm gone. Hopefully, we'll be closed tomorrow." Chip turns around, and as he's heading out turns and smiles at me. "Francie, do me a favor and turn my computer off before you leave...thanks."

"Let's call Charlottesville and make sure mom's alright. I can't imagine that she has forgotten my birthday. We were supposed to be going out for dinner. She had arranged for Lonnie, to care for her pets."

Jodi walks to my office and calls the sheriff in Charlottesville. She explains the situation as Sergeant and I pace back and forth in the small waiting area. Jodi returns to the waiting room with a tail wagging Bella.

"Francie, a deputy's going to make an attempt to go over to your mother's farm, if they are not able to reach her by cell or land line. Deputy Perkins has assured me that he will check on your mom. This storm is really hitting the mountains and Deputy Perkins said that calls are coming in continuously from folks without power, and individuals needing medical attention. The Red Cross has opened a shelter."

"Thanks Jodi."

"Why don't we walk over to Bill's and have a drink and eat something."

"I don't feel like it. Jodi, did you know that somebody dumped four foals in the pen over on Assateague and Elizabeth has them at her barn? I'm getting worried that something weird is going on again around here. First, this damn weather hits on

JIGSAW Teresa Adele Bettino

my birthday, and foals are abandoned, and now not hearing from mom."

"Francie, try to calm down. Maybe it is best if you close the agency, gather the dogs and go home to relax. I'm sure your mom's fine and will be calling you soon. How about if I give you a ring later?"

"That's fine Jodi. I'm so happy that you've returned to Chincoteague. It's been a hard year. I haven't recovered from the events of last year. I just hope mom's not in danger."

Jodi waits for me to walk to my office and turn off lights and my computer. Sergeant and Bella follow me knowing that something is up. I walk over to Chip's computer and turn it off. His office space is so neat and clean. What a difference from mine.

Jodi opens the agency door and the dogs run up and down the sidewalk. I hang the closed sign on the door as I slam it shut. The door always sticks, it's too large for its frame. Jodi heads for Bill's and I make a left and begin my slow trek up to Maddox. Sergeant and Bella are in heaven, frolicking in the snow. I walk as if I'm an old lady shuffling, head looking down fearing the worst with rounded shoulders. Every step is difficult as ice is the top layer. A combination of snow and ice pile into my mucking boots and I hold my shawl close to my face. This shawl smells like mom. Her love and care created it and it's my favorite possession. Within minutes, portions of my short curly hair are white and stiff with ice. As I turn onto Maddox, the wind freezes my face, making the hairs within my nose freeze. The feeling is uncomfortable and I bring my shawl to my nose. The dogs continue to run, getting rid of energy. I'm practically frozen by the time I reach my apartment. The steps are slippery and the dogs are eager to get inside the warm cozy apartment. I should have placed their winter coats on prior to leaving the agency, but I didn't. I'm feeling really scattered. Now their fur is soaked.

As I reach the top step, I open my backpack to locate my apartment keys. I locate the keys and as I'm fiddling with the lock, I can hear Sophie yowling. I open the door and Sergeant leads the way. Somewhere in my backpack my cell is ringing.

8

Cajun, Rick LaSlick, left New Orleans as the first drop of oil spilled. He knew the handwriting on the wall...the worst oil spill in history and didn't want his name involved. A gambling, thirty- year-old with a passion for art, Rick was a BP executive. Rick's good at figuring trends. Sometimes there's a shift to purchase land, sometimes stocks or mutual funds and sometimes just to sit, relax, and watch.

Rick doesn't want any ties to BP. He didn't want to make the mistake of saying too much or not doing enough like the CEO, who wanted his life back. Rick's proud of his Cajun roots and didn't want any linkage to this horrific oil disaster. Rick's full of pride that his great-great and so on great grandparents, aunts and uncles traveled from France to Nova Scotia in the early 1600's, and helped to build the first permanent settlement in Nova Scotia.

In reality, the LaSlick's got kicked out of; exiled, from Nova Scotia by the British. They traveled south arriving in Louisiana. Known as Acadians, Rick's ancestors settled in New Orleans making a living by fishing, trapping and boating. His great grandparents lived on a houseboat enjoying the rhythm of Gulf water, picturesque sunsets, and a healthy smell of fishy salt water.

His parents, Pierre and Marie Theresa, aunts and uncles are French Catholics who attend Mass and Holy Days. Tradition runs strong within his veins and Rick believes in hard work, obeying the Ten Commandments, attending church, and not having sex before marriage. The problem is that as an only overindulged child, Rick's developed bad habits. His belief's conflict with his actions as daily he uses rationalization as a means of comfort, combined with prayers for forgiveness.

Rick's a good liar, a gambler, who is addicted to money and sex. He enjoys escorts and dabbles in erotica. By attending confession weekly he feels absolved of his sins, especially sex prior to marriage. He believes that confession prevents him from getting hit by a bolt of lightning, and landing in hell. Rick thinks if he goes to purgatory that nobody will pray for him to get out and that he will bi-pass purgatory through prayer, confession and monetary donations. With his rationalism stretched to the max, Rick attends Mass, says his rosary prior to entering the confessional and prays to saints on their feast days.

He prays to Saint Francis Assisi, the patron saint of animals, as Rick enjoys off-track betting. On October 4, Saint Anthony's feast day, Rick says a special rosary for the horses that are running that day. Another saint prayed to is Saint Vincent de Paul, a French saint, known for his compassion of the sick and poor. For internal strength, Rick prays to Saint Michael the Archangel, to defend him against darkness and evil spirits and when he's feeling really crummy he prays to Guardian Angel Raphael for assistance with healing his colds, migraines and flu.

Prior to relocation, Rick studied the poor economy and the push for green. He centered his focus on the State of Virginia, it's on the east coast, and not too far from his parents. Rick developed four goals: new employment in the area of algae biofuels; purchase land within reach of brackish water; obtain again a six figure income and find a sex partner.

As Rick drove from New Orleans he contacted Exxon and Harbour Rentals, located on the Eastern Shore. He inquired about a vacant farmhouse in Bullbegger and then met Martha Smite, a local realtor. Rick was instantly attracted to this spot of the shore. Stepping into the old run down farm house, Rick became energized craving success and his first step was to renovate his new home, and his second, to become employed by Exxon. A view of the Bullbegger Creek and access to the creek, old family graves, six barns in good condition, fifty acres and the price was perfect, $250,000. He informed Ms. Smite on the spot that he wanted this place and paid $200,000 cash. Martha Smite found her lucky day and left with a signed contract.

After signing the contract, Rick spent his first night on the Eastern Shore at a bed and breakfast in Temperanceville. He likes history and spent some time reading about

Temperanceville. Rick finds it interesting that four men gave their land for a town center if folks agreed not to sell liquor. That certainly wouldn't happen in New Orleans. Rick downed a shot of Jack Daniels while sitting in the inn's living room. He smiled at this irony, belched and reached inside of his pants pocket for some Tums, as his acid reflux was kicking.

Rick decides to drive to Chincoteague, as he enters the island he is intrigued with billboards standing on the left side of the highway in marsh ponds. Driving over the modern bridge, with a full moon glistening over the Inlet, he opens his window and enjoys the smell of the bay. It reminds him of home. With hopefully a new career, and a farm contract, he's reaching his goals.

At AJ's on the Creek, a local restaurant, Rick sits at the bar and orders fresh crab with mixed greens and corn bread. A spicy Bloody Mary, Cajun style makes him feel at home. Beth, the bartender, makes a smooth drink and she's good looking. He wonders if she's loose enough to spend some time with him. Rick stays at the bar all night hoping to score with Beth. She has smiled at him throughout the evening and when Rick asks about a possible date, Beth throws back her head and laughs.

"What do you have in mind, Sonny?"

"Oh...I don't know...some companionship."

"We'll see. Let's see how the night goes. I don't get off until after two."

Rick continues to sit at the bar and mingle with Beth. He needs to score. This would make a perfect day. As he sits, he writes on a napkin, his to-do list. He plans to live downstairs in the living room, hire some cheap labor and start renovating the kitchen and bathroom. Get the chimney checked and purchase a wood stove. Winters, coming in a few weeks, although Virginia is a southern state, Rick's heard that it can have some snow and ice. Rick doesn't like the cold. He's never ice-skated or skied as a kid, even when his parents vacationed in the winter in Vermont over Christmas one year. They wanted to show their son snow. Rick didn't want any part of snow and cold so he stayed inside of the lodge watching television much to the displeasure of his parents.

At closing time, Rick follows Beth outside to the parking lot. Beth notices how drunk he is. Rick's too drunk to drive.

"I'll drive you to my place Sonny. You're too drunk to drive and will get stopped."

Rick walks around the Ford Escort to the passenger side, opens the door and collapses into the front seat. He hears Beth laughing. She drives down Maddox and over the bridge. Rick's too intoxicated to see the scenic view.

"Sonny, it's such a beautiful night. The moon's over the inlet and really brightening the sky. The stars look absolutely gorgeous." Beth looks over and Rick is sound asleep, his head's leaning against the window. She grins.

They arrive and Beth awakens Rick. "Come on, let's go in. It's too cold for me to leave you in my car. Rick moves, opens the door and weakly walks up to the house. With one wobbly foot in front of the other Rick arrives, and Beth escorts Rick to the living room. He sits on the sofa. Beth leaves walking into the hallway and returns with a pillow and blanket. "Sleep it off, Sonny." Beth says as she hands Rick his pillow and blanket.

"My name's Rick."

"You look like a Sonny-boy to me." Beth moves closer to Rick and pats him on the shoulder. "You're drunk and you can't be driving around here. You'll get popped on a DUI especially with Louisiana license plates. Sleep, is the best medicine. The bathroom's down the hallway and the kitchen is up the hall to the right. I'll see you in the morning, Rick. Good night."

Beth walks upstairs and Rick hears her bedroom door close. He flops onto the sofa, punches a soft spot into the pillow and covers himself with the wool blanket.

Meeting Beth two months ago was another goal achieved. Rick has a standing date with Beth, every Sunday. They attend mass at St. Andrew's and after church; walk the Stations of the Cross, a worn path, intertwined with flowers and graves, behind the church. The couple shares a late lunch at the Chincoteague Inn, enjoying sea food. Later in the day, they travel to Bullbegger, where Beth takes pleasure in studying the farm, inspecting renovations and admiring new finds of antiques that Rick has acquired. Beth's fallen in love with Rick's decoy collection and his kites from Kite Koop. He has them displayed outside, hanging from the numerous outbuildings, where bay breezes move each kite, adding unique sparkle to the colorful buildings. Exxon's paid for the barns to be renovated and converted to greenhouses, which have intrigued Beth. Tubs have been placed within each barn as water is piped from Bullbegger Creek. This enables algae to grow as the addition of sky lights has permitted the necessary light for a greenhouse effect. Beth's learned that algae grows faster than corn and can be used as fuel. Rick says it's the way of the future, unlimited fuel harvested within the United States. A green production, its win-win for the government and economy, with no dependence on foreign oil, and no greenhouse gasses going into the atmosphere.

Rick's happy as a clam. With renting his barns, and working for the company he's making about $200,000 a year. Not bad for a career change. His relocation to the Eastern Shore and an abrupt change in occupation is paying off. Rick's on the cutting edge and that's exactly where he wants to be.

I'm trying to answer my cell, which is in my backpack dangling over my shoulder. It's ringing as I fling open the door. I'm ready to relax as I'm over the day.

Sophie's right there at the front door for me to trip over. It's a ritual this tripping, as it occurs at least once or twice per week. The first trip is usually on a Monday morning when trying to use the bathroom after my alarm from hell has gone off. The second trip of the week is usually around food issues. Sophie has a thyroid condition and eats all day long. She whines, meows, stands in front of her empty food bowl until I give her a little bit more Tuna Select, the only food that she will eat and not regurgitate. The dogs have followed me and are busy shaking the remnants of snow off their coats. The apartment will stink in a matter of minutes; a combination of wet dog and Tuna Select.

I throw my backpack on the floor, open it quickly, and have missed the call. I scroll and ascertain that I've missed mom's call. I speed dial mom and... busy. Since old habits die hard, I walk into the kitchen, pull my grandmother's chair from the kitchen table, move it to the refrigerator, and stand on the chair grabbing my newest flea market biscotti jar, with bright reds and greens. I grab a packet of Twinkies, walk into the bathroom, open the drawer of my vanity, and neatly tucked inside of a Tampax box are several rolled joints. I rolled these about a week ago when I had purchased some pot. I light up...inhale...exhale and begin to relax. What a day this has been. I open the refrigerator and pour a glass of Chianti, cold the way I like it, take a bite of my Twinkie and a nip of wine. I'll have a good buzz going in a minute.

Sergeant and Bella are hungry so I feed them their food and Sophie gets a portion of Tuna Select. Everybody's happy. I decide to try and reach mom again.

On the third ring mom answers, "Happy Birthday, honey. I know that you probably think that I've forgotten your special day, but I've had a day from hell." *The apple doesn't fall far from its tree...*

"Mom, what's the matter as you do sound really stressed?" I exhale and take a swig of my wine.

"You wouldn't believe my day Francie. I feel like I'm back doing social work in Richmond. We're snowed in and this lady out of nowhere comes to my farm by way of taxi thinking that her son lives here. This lady fell from of the kitchen chair just as the lights went out. I managed to lift her off the kitchen floor, and have pulled a muscle in my lower back. We're still without electricity and I'm stuck with this demented soul as Charlottesville Social Services doesn't have a place to house her. They don't have any emergency homes."

I reach for my glass of Chianti and drink the rest. The joint is burning away in my ashtray. "Repeat what happened Mom, as you can't be serious. This is not your responsibility. Doesn't she have any relatives?"

Mom starts crying. I know that she's been really emotional these days as she's going through her change...night sweats, hot flashes and mood swings. "Mom, what can I do to help you?"

"There's really nothing anybody can do this very second. Nothing's moving here as we're snowed in.

"Mom who is this lady?"

"She's from New Orleans, has a son named Rick, and a husband Pierre that she says has been cheating on her. She says that there's some woman's clothing in her closet and that's why she left her husband. She refers to her husband as a "cheating bastard," Marie Theresa, that's this lady's name, says that she wants to live with her son and divorce her husband."

"Mom, how old is this lady?"

"Um...about eighty."

"And there are no emergency homes? I find it hard to believe that Charlottesville doesn't have any emergency homes."

"Nope...I'm stuck...this is your birthday and I wanted to see my only child."

Mom's crying hysterically, not a good sign.

"Mom, I think that you need a tranquilizer. Do you have anything to take for your nerves?"

"No...the only thing that I'm taking is a pill for my flashes, Premarin."

"Mom, are you nuts! When I took my health education course at VCU, the professor told the class that it's horse urine and to use herbs. I'll send you some information over the Net."

"What? No, the doctor didn't tell me anything. He just wrote a prescription. Some of my friends are on it and it's helping them with flashes, sweats and swings."

"Mom, use an herb, and get off it."

I inhale my jay as I walk into the kitchen; see my new biscotti jar and smile. I'm thinking of my ex-supervisor, Sally-Sue

Moon, who stole my Twinkies and pot filled Biscotti jar from Wanda Burton's desk, my mentally ill former co-worker. Sally-Sue got caught possessing it and is no longer my supervisor and is pulling time. I pour another glass of wine as mom's crying and I grab another package of Twinkies.

"Francie, why would the doctor give me horse urine? He knows that I own horses."

"Mom, you are so naive...I'll send you some information, alright?"

"Francie, I have to go. Mrs. LaSlick is calling me from the guest bedroom. I'll talk to you later. Have a nice birthday."

Mom hangs up and I walk to my computer and Google, *Premarin* and reach a site, *Premarin.org*. I begin reviewing... how disgusting... Mom's gonna flip when I send this. *Premarin*, meaning Pregnant Mares Urine... **P** for Pregnant, **M** for Mares, **U** for Urine, thus **PRE**gnant **MAR**es' Ur**INE** and for a shorter version, *PMU*. I e-mail mom, toke the rest of my joint, eat more Twinkies and decide to celebrate that my birthday's over as it's nearing twelve. Tomorrow's another day.

9

Jodi's Burgess, is sitting in a late afternoon meeting at the sheriff's department. Due to the four abandoned foals an emergency meeting has been called by the acting captain, Bill Nelson, who is more than ready to give up this taxing position to Jodi. His life hasn't been the same since he was told to cover for retired Captain Harold Winston. He wants no part of trying to figure out who the hell dumped these foals, especially during a blizzard...what a heartless bastard.

Greg Franks enters the room smiling. He's a happy fellow, thinking of Franice and knowing that he will spend the day with her tomorrow. After all she's depending on him and he aims to deliver. Snow, sleet or hail, isn't going to deter him. Greg notices Jodi sitting next to Bill. He puts two and two together and figures that Jodi's the new chief.

Jodi's a little nervous. After spending a year investigating cold cases, obtaining the position of captain is going to be a challenge...the head of the department, with much responsibility. Jodi's worked hard throughout her career. She desires change, however; is concerned with the "good old boy" mentality that is prevalent within predominately male departments.

Brittany's bubbly as usual. She's remained the center of attention, wearing a low cut sweater, tight black leather skirt, with black cowboy boots as her engagement diamond glistens from her perfectly manicured left ring finger. She's recently become engaged to Mike Griffin, and is his cowgirl. How Brittany has maintained the no wrinkle look working in such a stressful position is disconcerting to Jodi. Of concern to Jodi is how she and Brittany will mesh as Brittany is her administrative assistant. Jodi needs a trustworthy dependable person.

Jodi glances at her hands. The yellow diamond, a present to herself, purchased last year prior to her vacation with Francie to

Key West, looks plain compared to Brittany's diamond surrounded by rubies. Jodi looks up sheepishly as she listens to Bill Nelson's introduction.

"I'd like to thank everybody on the force for meeting on such short notice. As you are aware, we were supposed to meet tomorrow however; due to the abandoned foals and this blizzard we needed to touch base. As you can see, Jodi Burgess is present. Some of you will recall that she was employed by this department for a number of years, left Chincoteague for a supervisory position in Norfolk, and has returned. Well, she's back, trust me; I'm pleased to see her and to relinquish my acting title. Starting this minute she's our new captain. Um...Please welcome Captain Jodi Burgess."

Brittany drops her plate of cookies, picks up her fallen goodies and leaves the room brushing crumbs from her leather skirt. Greg Franks begins to clap his hands and whistle and Investigator Andy Walsh, who was Jodi's partner last year, walks to the table where Jodi's sitting and extends his hand.

"Welcome back Jodi, or should I say Captain," Andy says as he shakes her hand.

Other members of the sheriff's department walk to the table and congratulate Jodi. Jodi looks around the room, smiles and stands.

"Well, I just want to let everybody know that I've missed Chincoteague and am happy to be back. I know that we have many challenges ahead of us, and I also know what a good force and great folks you are to work with. I look forward to working with you. I believe in an open door policy. Please come by my office anytime."

Brittany returns to the meeting room with a faint smile on her face. Captain Burgess is ready to take command.

"As you know, four foals were abandoned at the Corral Pen. The foals were transported to Elizabeth Allen's farm over at Watts Estates near Wallops. As you know Warren McKinney is our newly hired animal warden. He's already commenced his investigation. Contact him for any questions that you may have.

He's going to be e-mailing status reports daily. You will review these reports during muster. Also, Molly Smith, our recently hired park ranger found a note about the foals after returning home from Assateague earlier today. She's contacted Warren who's reviewing the note and trying to make sense of it. He and I are meeting later today. At this time he's on his way to Elizabeth's farm to observe the foals and to take pictures. We need to be diligent. We need to find those responsible.

Elizabeth Allen's standing in the barn with her dog, listening to the howling winds and ice pellets hitting her metal barn roof. She's concerned as to the welfare of the four foals and is monitoring their food intake every few hours. Elizabeth's shocked that somebody dumped these foals at the Corral Pen. The foals, thank goodness, appear to be nibbling hay and nursing. Elizabeth's horse, Tiffany is contented as she has a foal to nurse again. Elizabeth is feeling better about this storm. She has checked gas containers and has plenty of gas for her generator in the event the electricity goes out. The barn won't lose power. Elizabeth's barn cat doesn't seem to care that there's a blizzard blowing about as she's nestled in some loose hay on the floor in the loft where hay is stored.

Elizabeth turns to leave the barn and she hears Princess growling. The barn door opens and it's Beth.

"I can't believe that you braved the elements."

"Well, I went home and rested a little and I keep looking out windows. My goats are fine. They're eating hay in a dry barn, so I thought that I would bundle up and trek over and see how everybody is doing. I hope that you don't mind?"

"No not at all. It gets pretty lonely around here when you can't get out and socialize. I guess you won't be working at AJ's for a few days?"

"I was finally able to reach the owner, and he's closed for the next few days. No big deal though Elizabeth as I have lots to do around the house. I can even paint a room if I feel like it. I purchased paint a few weeks ago for the guest bedroom, and haven't done anything yet. I have to be in the mood to paint."

"I know. Usually, my boyfriend James paints for me as he owns an odd-job company on Chincoteague."

"I didn't know that you had a boyfriend, Elizabeth?"

"It's a long story. Why don't we walk back to the house? We can drink hot tea or coffee. I'll cook some supper as I'm starved. Then I will explain or attempt to explain all that happened around here last year."

The women, brace for the weather as Beth opens the barn door. The wind whips down the isle of the barn, causing the horses to stir. Tiffany nostrils flare, her head goes up and tail follows... a typical Arabian.

Elizabeth picks up Princess as the snow is now above her shoulders and some of the drifts are hip height. They make their way slowly and reach the covered back porch steps. Elizabeth opens the kitchen door and walks in placing Princess on the kitchen floor's braided rug. Beth shuffles behind. Elizabeth starts a kettle of water for tea and makes coffee for Beth.

"So tell me about James and what happened last year before I moved here."

"Beth, has anybody ever spoken to you about The Legend of Horse Wind Chimes?"

"Nope. This almost sounds like the beginning of a Dean Koontz novel."

Elizabeth walks to the stove and pours boiling water into her teacup and places a mint tea bag into the water. She sighs. "I guess I better start with the legend."

Beth takes a sip of her coffee, and is sitting across from Elizabeth at the kitchen table. She's watching ice mixed with snow hitting the window...tap, tap, tap...as howling winds remain threatening.

"For us Eastern Shore folks The Legend of Horse Wind Chimes has been whispered for generations. Folk lore, legend, and myth are intertwined within our small communities. It's believed by some folks that when someone dies their soul needs something to attach itself to. Upon the person's death a wind chime, one of a horse, is attached by a loved one to the deceased, which serves as a portal. As the wind gently moves the attached chime, the soul of the deceased connects itself to this gateway. Legend has linked the wind chime to Chincoteague ponies as they have remained feral and have continued to have freedom of sea winds. This wildness coupled with their autonomy carries a loved ones soul to the next world."

Beth takes a piece of coffee cake and spots a bowl of popcorn and begins alternating eating both. Elizabeth notices that her eyes are wide, that her foot is shaking. She's anxious.

"This is really a good story Elizabeth. It's kind-of scary too."

"I know. There are lots of legends in this area. I'll continue. Just let me look out the window for a moment."

Elizabeth stands and walks over to the kitchen window. It's getting dark and she can see that it's still snowing. Winds have continued to make drifts about the farm. She returns to the table and grabs a handful of popcorn.

"Country folk believe in this legend and last year an elderly lady had horse wind chimes hanging from her tree. She didn't live too far from here, over at Helltown. The old lady's oak tree had many chimes, however; suddenly the chimes began to disappear from her tree, one by one."

"What the heck happened to them?"

"Well, this is where the story really gets tangled. Bart Connors, have you heard of him?"

"Yeah, wasn't he your neighbor?"

"Yes, he was my neighbor. During the period when folks were murdered and had a horse wind chime attached to them, I freaked out. One of my boarded horses was a victim of the Eastern Shore Wind Chime Killer. Bart lived next door to me and I depended on him to help me through this terrible time. James Parker, my boyfriend was going through a difficult period as he had fallen from a ladder. He shattered his leg, got hooked on pain pills and alcohol and basically lost it mentally. By the way, something of which I'm really proud of is that it was James' company, that built the new bridge.

"I really like the bridge. I've seen photos of the old one, which was really old world looking."

"I know. It was falling apart and we really needed a new bridge for islanders as well as tourists. I think that James' company did a good job constructing it.

"Driving over it is really picturesque; especially during a full moon with the light glistening off the bay."

"Does the bridge have a name?"

"I really don't know, Beth. I call it the new bridge."

"OK. Let's get back to this story. I think that it could be a best seller if somebody decided to write about it. Maybe Patricia Cornwell, as she lives in Richmond." Beth grabs more popcorn and takes a sip of coffee as sleet hits the window.

"Patricia Cornwell used to live in Richmond, moved to Manhattan and may have relocated again. I'm not sure. I do enjoy her books. Let me think of where I was...ah yes, James basically went nuts last year. He got addicted to pain pills, and drank. We broke up as Bart Connors and I started to get chummy. This really pissed James as he felt that I belonged to him. He was also concerned that Bart wasn't from here and that I didn't know a thing about him. The night that I told him to basically hit the road, he got furious, threatened to kill my dog if he tripped in another hole, drove to Chincoteague Island, and shot a Chincoteague pony that was stalled at the fairgrounds."

"Oh my God. That's really horrible, Elizabeth."

"I know. It's really been difficult for me to forgive him. He's pulling two years at the regional jail. Since he's dry and pulling his time, James is the person I fell in love with. He's found God and understands what happened. He's remorseful for his actions. Once he serves his time we are going to get married."

"That's a happy ending for you Elizabeth. Tell me what happened to Bart, what's his name?"

"Goodness...well Bart Connors, evidently hated social workers, followed Francie Batista and Jodi Burgess, who was a

Chincoteague investigator to Key West, Florida. Bart tried to kill Francie and wanted to kill her horse Trooper, which is boarded here. Bart was killed by the Key West police when he had Francie cornered in a shed. She had been shot in the shoulder."

"But why did he want to kill Francie?

"He hated social workers, and had wanted to kill Francie's horse, but shot the wrong horse. Bart had a troubled childhood and loved killing. He used to take the wings off of flies."

"That's really disgusting Elizabeth."

Elizabeth gets up from the table and excuses herself to use the bathroom. Princess follows her and waits. Beth gets up from the table, stretches; and her back cracks. She walks over to the kitchen door. The window panes are covered with ice. Beth is shocked about the harshness of this storm. This is worse than storms in New Jersey.

Elizabeth returns, grabs her cup of tea and stands by the sink staring outside. She seems to be deep in thought.

"Well, what happened next? And I thought that living on the shore would be quiet and carefree."

"It was far from that last year. Where did we leave off?"

"Elizabeth, I think we were at the part about Bart loving to kill and taking wings off of flies."

"Yeah...well he had a troubled childhood, loved money as he grew, depended on money for his gambling and was under the impression that he had a rich aunt. He stole the wind chimes from his aunt's tree, the lady that I just talked about, the one living in Helltown prior to his kill. Bart's plan was to take his aunt's money. He evidently believed in the legend."

"So why did he hunt Francie down in Key West?"

"He was a psychopath and obsessed about Francie. Francie and Investigator Jodi Burgess had been to his aunt's house as Francie had received an adult report. Bart figured that Francie was close to figuring out who the killer was. When Francie left for Key West with Jodi, I found a note hung on Trooper's halter. I freaked, called the sheriff's department who contacted Jodi.

Jodi had left Francie sunning at the pool and when she returned Francie was gone."

"Poor Francie. She has not shared with me what happened to her last year. Whenever I've seen her she looks so carefree."

"I know. She's a worrier though, especially when it comes to Trooper."

"I noticed how concerned she is about Trooper. I was in the kitchen earlier today when she called and I noticed how Russ downplayed Trooper throwing his shoe again."

"Yes, you're very observant. Francie hasn't been the same since last year. When Jodi left for Norfolk, she lost her best friend and support system. She's good friends with Jon and Jane. They own Sundial Books."

"Where's that place?"

"Oh, it's a classy book store on Chincoteague Island; it's located on the corner of Main Street across the street from the mall and theater."

"I'll have to look the place up some Sunday when I'm at church. Anyway, whatever happened to Bart?"

"Francie injured him with a hatchet, and he shot her in the shoulder. Then he fired at the police and was killed.

"Has Russ figured why Trooper keeps throwing his shoe?"

"The horse has stiffness with his back and periodically throws shoes. Russ is working on this. He has a friend, Charlie Scott who is a chiropractor. After the storm, Charlie's coming over to work on Trooper."

"Does Francie live by herself?"

"Yes, she has an apartment on Maddox. She has two rescue dogs that I think you've seen. They are Sergeant and Bella. Francie says that the dogs saved her life when someone attempted to break into her apartment."

"No wonder her nerves are shot...I don't blame her for having the dogs around and being tense. A lot of shit happens in Newark, high crime and murder rate, but you don't expect stuff like this to happen in Chincoteague and Watts Estates. I think with the passing of time, she will find peace and feel safe again."

Beth downs the rest of her coffee. "Elizabeth, if the electricity goes off can I spend the night? I don't want to be sleeping with the lights out, especially with the story that I've just listened to... The Eastern Shore Wind Chime Killer. It's too freaky. You know, this whole story reminds me of a jigsaw puzzle, where all the pieces touch, connecting."

"I know what you mean. Um...yeah, jigsaw puzzles, as in the end all of the parts interrelate."

Mike Griffin's inching his way to Temperanceville. This snow is one of the worst storms that he has seen in about ten years. Born in Chincoteague, Mike's been living on the shore since birth. He attended the local public schools, graduated and attended a local trade school. He's an air conditioner and heating repairman. He likes the money and enjoys screwing the customers, monetarily. Mike's in love with money and Brittany in that order. He's good at giving Brittany what she wants and good at putting her in place when she needs it. The bitch likes it that way.

He turns onto Route 13 and spots Brittany's car at a corner fast mart. He stops his truck and gets out, hopping into her car.

"What's up Brit?"

"What the hell's going on Mike? I heard about the foals and am wondering if you know anything about it?"

"What the fuck makes you think that?"

"Well, I know that you've been making money on the side and I want to know here and now if what's your doing is legal."

"Brittany, it's none of your business what I do, where I go and how I make money."

"It is, Mike. We're supposed to be getting married, if you recall...and I work for the sheriff's department."

"Shut the fuck up bitch."

"No I won't shut up."

Mike looks at her then backhands the bitch hitting her in the right eye. She screams, cringes, and starts crying. "Now, you have something to think about." Mike abruptly leaves, storming to his truck. He takes off heading south toward Temperanceville. He's pissed as he needs to deal with this asshole that dumped the foals. Life's about money and opportunity and Mike's found his niche.

Mike turns down the dirt road next-door to Cary Sadie Nation-Savages' house. He recently checked her heat pump, an annual maintenance check and although nothing was wrong with the unit, Mike told her that it needed a cleaning and charged the old coot three hundred dollars.

Mike drives to a large red barn, not seen from the road. This used to be the old hag's land, however; she sold it to Mary and Joseph Rigatoni, who live in New Jersey. They use it as a tax break and rarely visit, maybe for a month in the summer. Mary and Joseph have no clue what's up in their barn.

Mike parks, gets out, and inches his way to the barn's sliding door. He struggles to open it. The stench of manure is overpowering. He's in charge of cleaning and hasn't done so in a month.

"Hey Vince, you're here already. Where the hell did you park?"

Mike looks around. He sees another guy in the shadows. This dude comes out of the darkness. Mike squints. This guys muscular and smiling wearing a cashmere coat. He's overdressed for the shore with the long goat's wool coat.

"I hear that you have a problem about the foals."

"Yeah, I do and who the hell are you."

"I'm in charge here, not you and I'm your worst nightmare."

"What the fuck's going on?"

Mike's punched in the face, kicked in the ribs and falls to the floor. His hands are bound to his back with duct tape and a stinking rag's shoved in his mouth with tape holding it. He's carried to a stall and thrown in, discarded like a piece of shit. The men leave, closing the barn door. In the distance he hears a car starting. *Son of a bitch...what the hell's going on here...what the hell did I get myself into?*

10

Sally-Sue Moon's been sitting in the same stinky, dark cell in Goochland, Virginia for more than twelve months. Her marijuana possession charge was bogus. She feels framed and that it was probably Francie Batista or her mother, Gertrude. They're two peas in the same rotten pod as far as Sally-Sue's concerned.

Sally-Sue plans to find out who framed her. Why shouldn't she? She's been fired as a supervisor of social services, can't even apply for food stamps as she has a drug conviction. She will be released tomorrow. Juney Bea Karring, fired director of social services, for her less than honest hiring practices, and a friend of Sally-Sue's is traveling from New York City, to transport Sally-Sue to the eastern shore when she's released. Juney Bea's been employed by Bargain Basement of New York. Her position as buyer has enabled her to sort through garbage of the rich and famous living in apartments near Central Park. She runs a support group for welfare recipients called Dress for Success. Sally-Sue's intent on returning to the shore as she had prior to jail, purchased a small "Oyster home". It's an old home, set in a fishing village with plenty of sea gulls and shells. Sally-Sue loves collecting shells and enjoys making wreaths. Lots of tourists flock to the shore during the summer and love purchasing souvenirs. Sally-Sue has had plenty of time to think about a new career. Luckily, this past year she's had ample money in savings to pay bills. But one thing she's sure of, Sally-Sue is going to find out who framed her.

Rick LaSlick's sitting at his kitchen table, admiring a black and white photograph of an eastern shore gristmill. He's purchased this photograph from a guy he met sitting at AJ's bar, the other evening when Beth wasn't bartending.

That's when Rick was sipping a house wine and noticed this well dressed guy in a cashmere coat sitting a couple of stools away. They became drinking buddies, enjoying drinks, eating peanuts and watching the Cowboys and Eagles play. This newly found friend purchased Rick another glass of wine as he moved a couple of stools closer to Rick and the TV.

Rick takes another look at the eastern shore gristmill and smiles as he recalls what the guy said.

"I'm an Eagles fan. I'm from New Jersey and have season tickets."

"I'm not a fan of any football team. I really don't watch sports, except for horses running"

"Well, that's a sport, horse racing...the Triple Crown."

"I'd love to own a race horse. I enjoy betting. I haven't been to the track in New Kent County yet, but plan to. It's on my list of things to do. I've just relocated from New Orleans. Oh, by the way, my name's Rick LaSlick."

"Sal Rigatoni."

Rick catches the bartender's attention and orders another Bud for Sal.

"Thanks. Rick, do you like art?"

"Yeah, I have an appreciation and have walls at home, why?"

"Come outside. I have something to show you in the trunk of my car."

Rick smiles again recalling that Sal and he took their last swigs of drinks and exited the bar. Sal was parked in the back of the lot near sea grass and a brackish inlet. He opened the trunk and there were vases, pottery and photos. Sal placed these on the hood of his car. Rick admired and chose a black and white photo of an eastern shore gristmill. Rick studied the photo admiring the photographers eye.

"I like the black and white photo of a gristmill. It looks like it was taken around here."

"I don't know much about it. I'm asking two hundred."

"It looks pretty old. Oh what the hell, will you take a check?"

"No, I deal in cash. There's a Wells Fargo down the street."

Sal placed the remaining items in the trunk of his car and drove Rick to the bank. Rick handed Sal two hundred dollars. Sal smiled and shook Rick's hand. They returned to AJ's.

Once at AJ's, Rick got out of Sal's vehicle, then walked to the driver's side to say good-bye. "Well, thanks, Sal. I know that I'll enjoy this picture. It will look perfect in my renovated farmhouse. Maybe I'll be able to figure out who took it at some point. Are you staying for awhile before returning to New Jersey?"

Sal shakes his head. "Good-bye. Maybe our paths will cross again. It's been good doing business with you." The driver side window slides up as Sal leaves the parking lot.

Rick returned to his vehicle and sat for a few minutes admiring his new possession. The unframed photo could use a rustic thick natural wooden frame. Rick has plans to design a frame and hang this gristmill in his newly painted foyer. With natural light from the front door, this photo will surely add dimension to the foyer.

A contented Rick drove home and once home he continued to stare at his prize. As Rick's shaking his head, his cell phone rings, bringing him back to the present. It's his father, Pierre.

"Hey, Papa. Comment vas-tu?"

"Son, I can't find your mother?"

"Dad, what do you mean you can't find mom?"

"She's gone. She's been missing for about two days."

"What do you mean that she's been missing for two days? Have you called the police and filed a missing person's report?"

"Yes. I don't know what happened to your mother. She went to her closet to look for a dress and couldn't find what she was looking for."

"Dad, do you want me to come to New Orleans to help look for her? What do you mean that she was looking for something in her closet?"

"Well, lately she's been a little forgetful and distant. I just thought she was going through something female. But when she went into our closet to look for her dress and couldn't find it, she said that it was another woman's clothing in our closet."

"What!"

"Your mom then put something else on, grabbed her alligator pocketbook and said that she was meeting Jean Marie for lunch. She never met Jean Marie for lunch and didn't return home. So I called the police and filed all the necessary paper work."

Rick gets up from the kitchen table with his cell phone plastered to his ear. He goes directly to his whiskey bottle and pours himself a stiff one. Takes a gulp, stops breathing for a second and returns to the kitchen table where he proceeds to flop into the chair.

"Dad, I'm in the middle of a major snow storm and probably won't be able to get there for a couple of days. What's the name of the investigator who's in charge of mom's case?"

"Oh, it's a man named Louis; I don't have his professional card in front of me. I'll call you back."

Pierre hangs up and Rick's numb, he can't feel his hands around his whiskey glass. *Mom's missing...I can't believe this shit.*

Jodi Burgess is sitting at her desk. She's trying to make herself feel comfortable in this masculine office. There's the stuffed head of a buck hanging from the far wall staring at her with deep black sad eyes. She shutters looking at the poor victim, of someone else's pleasure. Behind her is a large window. She turns her chair around and stares at the snow mixed with ice.

Jodi hears someone enter her office; she turns her chair to face the door. It's Andy Walsh, her ex-partner.

"I just want to say congratulations. I've really missed working with you."

"I know. Last year, we worked hard to find the killer. It was a crazy time as I had paid for a vacation and was not about to lose my money. How are you and Linda?"

"We're fine. She's pregnant and due this spring."

"That's wonderful. And how's little Sammy."

"He's not little any longer. He says that he's going to be a big brother. In September Sammy will be entering Kindergarten."

"Time really flies. I'm happy to be back. I missed the adrenaline rush, around here. Cold cases were a lot of desk time, reading and studying old information. It takes a special person to sit and sift through a lot of paperwork."

"Well, you are a special person Jodi. I'm pleased that your back. Linda and I will have to invite you over for dinner one night to celebrate. How about if we plan to get together after the holidays?"

"Wonderful. And thanks for asking, partner."

Beth's staring at snow and ice, which has layered on her windows. She's drinking a screwdriver and is feeling sorry for herself. The house is quiet and she's listening to a newly acquired grandmother's clock located in the foyer...tic...tock...tic...tock. What would she be doing in Newark? Escorting, and partying. Maybe buying this farm was the wrong decision. It's so lonely when you can't get out of your road and you're up to your ass in snow. Who knew that Virginia had winters like this? She takes a sip of her drink, closes her eyes and is reminiscing about her childhood. Was Newark so bad? Beth misses her cousins and neighborhood. How many Greeks live on the eastern shore? She takes another sip, gets up and walks over to her CD's. She looks through them and there's nothing that she really feels like listening to. Beth walks over to the living room window. Coming down her dirt road is a red truck. It's Rick LaSlick.

Sally-Sue Moon's reading the final chapter of Dr.'s Paul Babiak and Robert Hare's *Snakes in Suits*, as an avenue to help with the passage of time. Anticipating freedom is giving her rushes that she had forgotten that she could feel. Her heart's racing. She's hopeful that Juney Bea has left New York City and has traveled to Goochland as planned. Of all the days for it to snow, today and tomorrow isn't one. Juney Bea's supposed to reserve a room for the night at the local Holiday Inn.

Sally-Sue's acquired this rather interesting book from the jail's library. With every word read, she's thinking of Francie Batista and her worthless mother, Gertrude. Both are snakes in the grass. Having attending Virginia Tech with Gertrude and knowing Gertrude in the late sixties, she knows Gertrude has smoked pot. Sally-Sue's feeling pretty confident that the pot in the Biscotti jar was Gertrude's. After all Gertrude was sitting at Wanda Burton's desk. Sally-Sue saw Gertrude rummaging through Wanda's desk when she opened the agency's front door.

Sally-Sue is speed reading and agrees with the authors. There are snakes in the work place. Sally-Sue is becoming increasingly agitated. She was screwed by the court process, her sentence, and framed. She's narrowed the playing field. The person or persons that screwed her were the Batista's. Both fit the definition of work place psychopaths. Sally-Sue reads a portion of the book's last sentence out loud. "Sometimes you just have to cut out the deadwood." Sally-Sue smiles as she looks to the ceiling, and closes her eyes thinking of sweet dreams.

11

A new day, thank God to be over my so-not birthday. The sun's rising, no snow is falling and in the distance I hear Sammy, as his snowplow's humming along side streets. I'm up and out of my apartment by nine, with the dogs. There's no need to rush, county offices are closed although I feel compelled to check on the wellbeing of the adults in my two new reports.

One report relates to an elderly man named Bryon Cloud, who resides by himself and isn't bathing. The other reports about an elderly woman named Cary Sadie Nation-Savage. She's the woman who claims to have been in a Ron Jeremy porno flick. *Ah, such is life...*

I'm schlepping to my office as Sergeant and Bella race madly about. It's cold. Of course the dogs love the drifts and are running at full speed as we proceed down Maddox to Main. The snow remains over my mucking boots, so I have large plastic dark green garbage bags tied above my knees. I walk covering my face with my brown wool shawl that mom designed. My shoulders are hunched over, head down, and breathing deeply makes me appear old and haggard. Nothing's moving on Chincoteague Island. There are no cars, going anywhere. We're walking in the middle of the street as I am trying to step in the snowplow tire tracks. What a difference a day makes.

We make a left onto Main Street and continue to make our way slowly to the agency. Arriving, a large drift has formed in front of the door so I take my foot and start to move the snow over so that I can open the door. Once the door is opened, Sergeant and Bella run in ahead of me. I shut the door, lock it and proceed to walk through the waiting room, passing Chip's desk to my cluttered back room office. I'm thankful that we didn't lose electricity as it's nice and toasty. Since county offices are closed, I'm not going to announce that I'm here. My intent is to contact Greg Franks and hitch a ride with him on these two adult cases.

Sitting at my desk, eating a chocolate granola bar and day old cold coffee, I'm reviewing the report on Bryon Cloud. He lives on the mainland not far from Cary Sadie Nation-Savage in Parksley. Since Ms. Nation-Savage lives in Temperanceville I'll interview her last as I return to Chincoteague. The phone rings.

"Hey Francie... Greg. I've made it to work and have the 4-wheel drive warming as we speak. I'm ready to take you where you need to go today. I cleared it with the boss, Captain Burgess."

I smile. *The cats out of the bag...she's in charge.*

"Ok. I'll meet you in front. Just honk when you get here so that you don't have to get out in the elements. I'm going to write a short note to Chip in case he comes into work to inform him of my whereabouts. I'll leave Sergeant and Bella in my office. They're tired from walking in the snow and will sleep for the better part of the day."

Gertrude Batista is up and about, feeding horses and giving her dog, Buddy his breakfast. The snow has finally stopped and is glistening on fir trees as the first rays of sun shine on frozen snowy branches, the barn, and woods. She walks from the barn with Buddy at her heels. Her intent is to check on Mrs. LaSlick and to call her son, Rick. Last night with the whiteout she was unable to call. Her cell wouldn't work. Gertrude spent the night awake, alert just in case Mrs. LaSlick began to wander or was nuts. Gertrude had visions of Mrs. LaSlick walking into the kitchen, finding a knife and proceeding to slice her into little pieces. Hey what the hell, shit happens. She doesn't want to be one of the statistics at the end of the year, a picture on *The Today Show.*

As she's walking towards the house, Gertrude notices the antique lace curtain in the guest room moving. She can see the image of Mrs. LaSlick, staring outside. Buddy runs ahead and is on the front porch waiting as Gertrude trudges on. Gertrude's happy that the snow isn't as bad as anticipated; it looks as though Richmond and areas east got hit harder than the mountains. Hopefully the cell is working.

As Gertrude and Buddy walk into the foyer, Mrs LaSlick is dressed and coming down the stairs.

"Hi Mrs. LaSlick. Good morning. Did you get a good night's sleep?"

"Yes, I did honey. Are you Rick's wife?"

"No. Mrs. LaSlick, I'm not your son's wife. We went over this yesterday. Do you remember that you came here by taxi thinking that your son lived here?"

"He does live here honey."

"How about if we have some breakfast? I'm going to call your son today. I'm hopeful that my cell phone will work now that the storm is over and the sun is out."

"OK dear."

Gertrude and Buddy walk into the kitchen following Mrs. LaSlick. She proceeds to sit in the same old Oak chair that she fell from yesterday. Gertrude starts the gas burner and gets the eggs out of the refrigerator. She cracks a couple, adds a little milk, and scrambles some eggs on a greased fry pan. The wheat bread's toasting as Gertrude pours some orange juice in a glass for her uninvited houseguest. Once the bread is toasted and eggs cooked, Gertrude places breakfast on a plate with a sliced orange.

"Well, thank you. This is really nice. I'm so pleased that my Rick married a girl that knows how to cook. I've been wondering when Rick and you are going to have a baby. I would love to have a grandbaby."

This woman is nuts...I might be feeling nuts because I'm menopausal, deep into hot flashes, and mood swings. However; I know what day of the week it is and that I'm not married and am not going to have a baby.

I hear Deputy Greg Franks give a honk, grab my reports and a notebook, say good-bye to the dogs and proceed out the front door. As I'm about to get into the truck, I notice one of the feral cats trying to walk down Main Street to his food bowl behind the agency.

"Greg, can you wait just one minute. I forgot to leave some food for the island's cats. I'll be right back. I don't want to hold you up, as I really appreciate your driving me around today."

"It's no problem. I'm enjoying it Francie as it gets me out of completing paperwork."

I jump out of the vehicle, and quickly re-open the agency door. As I look up Main Street, I notice Chip coming to work. His head's down and he's bundled up for the elements."

"Chip, hey...it's me!"

I push the door, walking in as Chip follows. Sergeant and Bella eagerly greet us at the door, tails wagging.

"Chip, I'm about to feed the feral cats. I've written you a note, as I'll be out in the field with Greg Franks. I'm surprised you came to work since offices are closed."

"I have lots of work to do and thought that it would be productive to come in, have no women sitting in the waiting room and attempt to get caught up."

"Can you keep an eye on the dogs for me?"

"Yeah, no problem. I'll walk to Sundial to say hi to Jon and Jane as we'll go stir crazy after a few hours."

"That's great. Thanks so much."

I walk to the kitchen, pour some dry cat food in a bowl and can barely open the kitchen door due to the gathered snow. I retrieve a shovel from the kitchen closet and struggle to make a small clearing. Once completed…cats start coming out for food.

I return, pass Chip where the dogs are sitting next to his desk and proceed to walk from the agency. Greg's waiting patiently. I sigh and get into the car…exhaling a breath of relief. Greg starts moving forward, makes a U-turn in the middle of Main and we slowly inch our way to the new bridge.

"OK, the first person that we're going to see is Bryon Cloud. He lives alone and is self-neglecting. The caller reported that he hasn't been bathing. He lives over in Parksley and the other report, the lady lives in Temperanceville, so I thought that we would go to the furthest place first, if that's alright."

"No problem."

"Mr. Cloud lives off of Dunne and I bet he lives in one of those old Victorian houses. I hope that he isn't a hoarder. I'm so sick of all these old folks, saying that they're collectors and their place smells, hasn't been cleaned in years and has junk piled to the ceiling."

As we creep along, the glare from the snow mixes with the sun and is blinding. Greg's squinting as he doesn't have sunglasses on. He puts the sun visor down to help lessen the intensity.

"Greg. You're struggling to see. Do you want to use my sunglasses?"

"If you have a spare, I'd appreciate it. I don't want to take the ones that you're wearing Francie as you need them too."

"I don't have an extra; you can use these since you're driving."

I hand Greg my black sunglasses and pull down the visor on my side. The snow's blinding. We continue slowly along. The extent of the blizzard is visible with drifts, power lines down, and bent fir trees. Luckily, the Virginia Department of Transportation has been working diligently throughout the night."

"So Jodi's your captain? What do you think of that Greg?"

"I'm fine with it Francie and happy for her. She's worked hard and deserves the opportunity to be in charge. I think that she will be fair to her subordinates."

"I agree. She's my best friend. Jodi has been referring to me as her partner in crime for a couple of years…and I think that we worked well together when we completed investigations. I am happy for her that she's achieving her goals."

Greg turns right onto Dunn and we start to count houses. I'm usually able to "tell" which house I'm going to be visiting without looking at numbers. I hate to say that, stereotyping; but I've gotten good at it. We soon zone in on Bryon Cloud's house. It's on the left, a Victorian type that appears to be in pretty good shape. There's a plastic Santa on the porch waving. Nice touch, kind-of tacky, but at least he's in the spirit. Greg stops the vehicle and we get out and slide our way to the front porch. Greg holds onto me as we attempt what appears could be where the steps are. We make it and Greg gives a good knock on the front door, while I grope around for the doorbell. We hear shuffling to the front door. The door opens slowly on a crack.

"Hello, sir. Are you Bryon Cloud?"

"Yes, what is this about?"

"Well, sir, I'm Francie Batista with social services and Deputy Franks is with me as I can't drive in this weather. Someone called and wanted me to check on you. Can we come in for a few minutes, its cold out here?"

Bryon Cloud opens the door and permits us in. He is unkempt looking. PJ's too large, a bit dirty with tattered slippers, which were probably once light brown suede now black with big toe holes. We follow Mr. Cloud into his living room. It is dark, cluttered, and needs a good cleaning. Dust is layered. He turns on a light. In the corner is a television with a recliner in front and a tattered sofa near to the right. I see that he's watching Michael Jackson's *Thriller*. Mr. Cloud walks over to the sofa and sits. I sit next to him. Greg stands, watching *Thriller*.

"Um...Mr. Cloud, I explained, "I'm with social services and I'm out here to check on how you are doing. It's part of our community service program for elders."

"Who called you?"

"Someone who is concerned as to your welfare, sir. I'm not at liberty to give you the name of the person. I'd like to ask you a couple of questions Mr. Cloud."

"OK."

"Can you tell me if you have eaten breakfast this morning?"

"No. I just got out of bed."

"Did you eat dinner last night?"

"I did eat. I used to be a cook for the army during the big one. I cooked for a couple of hundred men."

"Can you tell me what you made for yourself last night?"

"I made meat loaf with baked potatoes."

"Oh that's really nutritious. Do you know what year this is?"

"1943."

I have all that is needed. He's demented and self-neglecting. Basically this is a slam-dunk investigation.

"Sir, do you have any relatives that live here or somebody that checks on you?"

"Can't say that I do. I have a daughter, Maggie that lives in Norfolk."

"Do you know her phone number?"

"It's on the refrigerator door."

"Is it OK if I walk into the kitchen to look for it?"

"Yes, you can Missy. What is this all about? I'm getting confused as to your purpose."

"As I said, Mr. Cloud, I'm a social worker and check up on the elderly especially when there is a snow storm. Some caring person called and wanted me to check on you."

I get up and make a quick exit. I look over at Greg who's rolling his eyes and watching *Thriller*. I notice that he is bobbing his head to the music. Mr. Cloud's also bobbing, although to a different beat.

I open the refrigerator door and see that there's very little food. No meatloaf and I open a carton of sour milk. It takes my breath away. I look on the refrigerator door and see some names in large letters followed by large numbers. His physician is Dr. Henry Walker. My plan is to call Dr. Walker. I will also speak with Maggie, his daughter, who is also the complainant. We'll need to come up with a safe plan of care for Mr. Cloud so that he can continue to live alone. This is really a high risk situation.

I walk into the living room, and Greg's continued to watch television. Mr. Cloud's sitting in his recliner directly in front of the TV.

"Mr. Cloud, do you like the video *Thriller?*"

"Yes, ma'am. I'm one of the dancers."

Greg shifts his body weight to his right leg and brings his hand to his mouth. I smile. "Mr. Cloud, how about if I make you some breakfast and I'll bring it to you so that you can eat while you watch Michael Jackson? Are you on any medications?"

He doesn't answer so I return to the kitchen, find some bread and eggs and proceed to cook a couple of eggs with toast and jelly. I locate an apple, slice it and put it on a plate with the toast and eggs. I note that dishes are dirty in the sink, so he has been eating. I'm wondering what condition the bathroom is, so I decide to take a look after I give him his food. I find some instant coffee. He's going to have to drink it black as I've thrown the milk in the trash. The trash is full and nasty so I open the back door and throw the plastic bag out. His daughter can come over and put the trash in the garbage can. That is if she can find the bins. I find another plastic bag and place it in the trash receptacle. I locate one of those old 1950's TV dinner trays folded in the corner of the kitchen, unfold it, clean it and place the food on it.

I return to the living room with food and place the tray in front of Mr. Cloud. He eagerly starts eating. I leave the living room and locate the bathroom. The tub is filled with last year's newspapers, along with garbage bags and some canned food. I check the medicine cabinet and don't see any medications and return to the living room. Greg's now leaning on his left leg, no longer bobbing and has moved across the living room and is staring at the wall with a blank expression on his face. Mr. Cloud gobbles his eggs and gulps his black coffee.

"Mr. Cloud, I have your phone number and I will be getting back with you later today. Have you ever heard of Meals on Wheels?"

"Ma'am, I'm a cook and make meals for hundreds of hungry men. I don't need hand-outs."

"Well, Mr. Cloud I'll call you later. Deputy Franks and I need to leave as we have someone else to visit."

He waves goodbye, and is merrily contented eating apple slices with his best friend, Michael Jackson as we shut the front door.

"Greg, I'll need to contact his daughter today as Mr. Cloud is high-risk. He's living alone and not taking care of his basic

JIGSAW Teresa Adele Bettino

needs.   I don't think that he's using his bathroom near the kitchen; hopefully he has another one somewhere within the house and isn't hiking to relieve himself."

12

Captain Jodi Burgess is nestled at her desk reading the local newspaper, the *Chincoteague Beachcomber*. It's about nine in the morning the day after the blizzard and she's in a better mood as she spent yesterday getting rid of the Chief's clutter. She needed to make his office her own. Jodi loves decorating so last night while at home she rummaged taking knick-knacks for her office such as; pictures of her friends, a red depression era glass vase with dried roses, of red and white. She's brought to the office a couple of red pillows and a few plants to make the office less dreary. Jodi enjoys giving and treating herself. She loves jewelry especially the yellow diamond ring that she purchased last year as a gift to herself when she was going on vacation to Key West, Florida. She spends a second admiring her yellow diamond, placing her right ring finger under her desk lamp. *If I make it as captain for one month, I'm going to watch the QVC channel and treat myself to another piece of jewelry. It's the bling in life that keep me centered, happy and healthy.*

Jodi's in a better frame of mind today with the snow ceasing. Sammy's plowing streets and life is getting back to normal, whatever normal is on Chincoteague Island. She's decided not to overwhelm herself. Focus on what's necessary and have a positive outlook. Making her office her own was her first step in conquering her fears as Captain.

Jodi earlier this morning moved her desk to face the window. She struggled, strained and cursed as she used her body to shove and push this solid wood desk. Jodi's well aware of security and knows that this is a big, no-no. Somebody could come from behind and whack her. She's doesn't care, as she needs to feel comfortable. For this moment in time, Jodi's elated as she owns this office now. It no longer belongs to the Chief.

Jodi's staring outside. In the distance she sees someone walking, head down, shoulders rolled forward, with two dogs running alongside. *That's got to be my best friend in life, Francie Batista.* Jodi, giggles watching Sergeant and Bella nearly knocking Francie over as she walks towards the department of social services. Francie's wearing her mucking boots and her brown wool shawl. She's using part of the shawl, to cover her face. *Poor Francie, how she hates the winter... I do hope that she had a good birthday...don't think so though.*

Jodi turns and faces the door as in the distance she hears Brittany entering the hallway to her office. As she turns, Jodi notes how lovely her office appears. Pictures of local artists are displayed especially in the area where the buck was hanging. There's a work of local art by Rose Taylor, entitled *Chincoteague Ponies* as there are three ponies in angry surf moving in unison. It's absolutely breathtaking. Jodi's elated that the buck's found a new home. She gave it to Deputy Cindy Franks, who was delighted. Her husband's a deer hunter, although hasn't killed a deer. She said that she was going to surprise him for Christmas. He'll be able to spin a tall tale now.

Jodi turns her chair again and is looking at Main Street. Francie's nowhere visible. Jodi glances down and catches an article on the front page of the newspaper. She's interested in an article that appears in the *Washington Post*. It's about a woman named Frances Benjamin Johnston, a deceased photographer who once took photos of interesting places on the Eastern Shore. She took pictures of old farmhouses, log cabins and unique dwellings and structures. This took place in the 1930's. At some

106

point Frances donated her photos to the Library of Congress and evidently a heist of her photos happened a week or so ago.

Animal control officer Warren McKinney's making his way slowly to Elizabeth Allen's horse farm to interview Elizabeth and to check on the welfare of the foals. He attempted to visit with Elizabeth during the blizzard, however; returned to Chincoteague after receiving a call from Ranger Molly Smith When he arrived at her house, she presented him with a note that had been attached to her door. He's memorized it, however; is having difficulty attempting to figure out the meaning.

Temperanceville foals began
Pony Corral's their end
Hurry, Park Ranger
Danger.

It's Wednesday about nine in the morning as Warren turns onto Elizabeth Allen's dirt road. He sees her shoveling a snow trail to her barn. He sees snowdrifts, and watches as Elizabeth vigorously uses her shovel to break through one in order to make a straight path from the house to the barn. Warren gets out of his jeep and makes his way to Elizabeth, whose stopped working, breathing hard and looking at him.

"Hi. Elizabeth Allen?"

"Yes. I assume that you are the newly employed animal warden Warren McKinney?"

"Yes, you got that right. Let me help you shovel a little and then we'll make our way to the barn to visit with the foals. How are the foals doing, Elizabeth?"

"Well, I checked on them throughout the night. They're eating like there's no tomorrow."

"That's a relief that they're going to make it... the fact that they have been accepted by the nannies and your horse...um...what's your horse's name?"

"Tiffany, she's a wonderful horse, a little flighty at times being an Arabian. She lost her foal, and was still full with milk, so this is a match made in heaven. She's really nurturing her baby and is permitting the foal to nurse whenever it wants."

Warren continues shoveling. "Now I understand why folks have heart attacks shoveling. This is really hard work and I'm in relatively good shape."

"I know. I thought that I was going to faint yesterday during the blizzard as I was trying to keep ahead of the buildup. I shoveled for about twenty minutes, and then rested. This is too much snow. I'm not used to this kind of weather. Let the State of Maine have snow, not the sunny south."

Warren reaches the barn and shovels an area around the barn doors. He opens the door and he and Elizabeth enter. Warren notes how clean and organized Elizabeth's barn is. All the horses have fresh shavings; bales of hay stacked upstairs, clean water buckets and feed bins.

"During feeding time, I walk upstairs, gather a flake or two of hay and throw it down to the occupied stall. The horse knows to move out of the way." Elizabeth says with a chuckle.

Warren sees wheel barrels with manure mixed with shavings. It's apparent that Elizabeth's been tossing manure, out the barn's back doors.

"You keep a really clean and organized barn, Elizabeth. I wish that all the folks who have livestock kept their animals like you do. You're to be commended especially with this kind-of weather."

"Thanks so much. I really love the life that I have although at times it has been a hard road."

They travel up and down the aisle with Princess walking next to Elizabeth. Warren bends down to pet the barnyard cat. "I bet she's a good mouser."

Elizabeth giggles, and walks up the steps tossing additional hay. She returns and checks the level of water in buckets. Warren takes photos of the foals and shakes his head.

"I'm trying hard to figure out who in God's name would abandon four foals in the middle of the worst blizzard in the last ten years. Somebody's left a note about it on the door of Park Ranger Molly Smith's house."

"Really, can you tell me what it said?

"Yeah...maybe your insight can help with the investigation. It said Temperanceville foals began, Pony Corrals their end, Hurry Park Ranger, danger."

"Well that doesn't make much sense. I'll tell you what you need to do is to contact Francie Batista as she is really good at investigations and placing pieces together. Have you heard about The Eastern Shore Wind Chime Killer?"

"Yes, Molly explained to me what happened last year."

"Well, Francie kept telling her friend Investigator Jodi Burgess that she felt that the chimer was out to get her. She gets these *feelings* as she calls them...almost like a sixth sense...like a shiver up her spine. I bet she could help you with this. You know she is also an investigator of children and adult abuse."

"Yes, I'd heard that she works for social services and investigates abuse and neglect. That's a good idea. Thanks and I'll contact her when I return to Chincoteague."

They leave the barn and are heading to the house when they spot Beth attempting to walk over from her place. She's all bundled for the weather and breathing hard. There appears to be a man walking along side of her."

"Hi everybody."

"Hi Beth. Do you know the new animal warden Warren McKinney?"

"No...but I do now. Glad to meet you, I'm Beth Keller. I'd like to introduce you to a friend of mine. He arrived late last night to check on me.   Elizabeth and Warren this is Rick LaSlick."

"Nice to meet everybody."

"Would you like to come inside and warm up as I've made some cornbread this morning and have brewed some fresh coffee?"

As Elizabeth opens the kitchen door, Princess rushes past everyone followed by Warren, Beth and Rick eager to become warm. The wood stove has really made the house comfortable with the smell of wood and aroma of freshly brewed coffee. The sweetness of freshly baked corn bread adds to this delight.

"Warren and I were just about to attempt to figure out a note left on the park ranger's door yesterday.   The words are puzzling. We can't imagine who would have left these babies to freeze to death. Rick, has Beth shared with you what happened on Assateague Island?"

Rick shrugs his shoulders and looks over to Beth, whose sitting at the table drinking coffee and eating corn bread. "No, what's happened?" Rick says as he reaches over Beth's head for a piece of corn bread. He walks over to the kitchen table, slides a chair next to Beth's and pours some coffee.

"Yesterday, during the storm, four foals were abandoned on Assateague. They were left to die in the Corral Pen. Molly Smith, our park ranger discovered them. I was contacted and requested to provide help so I spoke with Beth as she has goats. Horses can survive on goat's milk. Doug Fields, a Salt Water Cowboy thought of using goat's milk as he's knowledgeable about equines. Lucky for me, Tiffany, my horse, still had milk from losing her foal a couple of months ago so she's nursing one of the foals."

"What does the note say and perhaps we can figure this out. It is unspeakable that someone did this. Rick looks at Beth who has her head down.

To answer your question Rick, this is what the note said. "Temperanceville foals began, Pony Corral's their end. Hurry, Park Ranger, danger."

"That's really strange. I know a little about Temperanceville, as I stayed at a bed and breakfast and read about the town. As far as the foals, I think that the person who wrote the note is pointing you to this community." Rick's cell rings...he removes the cell from his back pocket, looks at the number and shakes his head. "I think that I better answer this as my mother's missing." He abruptly pushes his chair away from the table, takes a swig of coffee and walks towards the hallway leading to Elizabeth's living room.

Beth, Warren and Elizabeth eye each other. "He never told me that his mother's missing. I'm in shock. How can his mother be missing and he's able to function? This is absolutely unreal!"

Rick continues through the hallway and finds Elizabeth's cozy living room, a room with old Victorian rocking chairs mixed with wicker. A gentle fire's warming the room as bright sunlight streams through laced antique curtains."

"Hello."

"Hi. Is this Rick LaSlick?"

"Yes. This is he and to whom am I speaking?"

"Sir, I am Gertrude Batista and am calling from Charlottesville, Virginia. Your mother showed up at my farm thinking that you live here. She spent the night with me due to the weather and I am trying to come up with a plan in order to transport her to you. She is confused and therefore would be at risk to travel alone. I'm a retired social worker so I'm pretty good at problem solving. Where do you live?"

"I live in Bullbegger, near Temperanceville, Virginia."

"That is fantastic as my daughter; Francie Batista is a social worker in Chincoteague. This is really good luck for us as yesterday was her birthday and I planned, prior to the snow of course, to visit with her. I will leave for the Eastern Shore tomorrow. I will transport your mother to the social services agency located in Chincoteague. I will call Francie and request her presence. How about if we meet at three in the afternoon? Would you like to speak to your mother?"

"Yes. Certainly."

Gertrude hands the phone to Rick's mother. He's thankful that his mother has been located, however; concerned that his mother left New Orleans thinking that his father had been cheating.

"Bonjour maman. Comment allez vous?"

"Bonjour Rick. I'm fine, bien, son. Why aren't you here? I like your farm house."

"Mom, you're a little bit confused. I will see you tomorrow. I love you."

Marie Theresa returns the cell to Gertrude.

"As, I said, Mr. LaSlick, your mother is very confused. She thinks that I'm married to you. I will contact Francie and we'll see you tomorrow."

Rick leaves the living room and returns to the kitchen. Everybody's silent and has a bewildered look. Eyes look at the linoleum. Rick breaks the silence.

"Who knows a social worker named Francie Batista?"

Elizabeth smiles, "We do. Her horse Trooper is boarded here. Why?"

"Evidently, my mother traveled from New Orleans to Charlottesville thinking that I resided in a farm house owned by, Francie Batista's mother, Gertrude Batista. She's bringing mom to Chincoteague tomorrow. I'm to meet with Francie Batista, her mother and my mother at Francie Batista's office. Do you know where it is located?"

"It is a small building between the library and Sundial Books on Main Street across from the Village Mall. It's a painted brick building small in stature. You'll know it when you see it, as the

building is old and has the "look" of a social services building."
Warren says with a chuckle as he pops a piece of corn bread into
his mouth smacking his lips.

"What do you think Francie Batista's going to do about my
mother's situation?"

Elizabeth gets up from the table. She walks to the kitchen
sink and is looking at the barn. She turns to Rick, "Francie's
mother is a retired social worker and she will speak to her
daughter about your mother's welfare. Francie will want to talk
to you about your mother's situation and how she can help."

This is really a messy situation. "I really need to get going.
My father has contacted the New Orleans police and filed a
missing persons report. Some phone calls are necessary. I am
thankful that my mother has been located and is safe."

Beth gives a smile and takes a sip of her coffee discarding the
remains into the kitchen sink. She gives Princess a quick pat and
looks at Elizabeth as she and Rick make a quick exit.

"Wow that was different. I wonder why Beth hasn't
mentioned Rick to me as we're pretty close friends. I wonder
why he moved from New Orleans to Bullbegger, as I heard him
say."

13

Sally-Sue's ready. She's clutching her new read, *Snakes in Suits*, as she walks through the jail to the last locked door leading to her freedom. She's changed into her street clothes. The purple linen pantsuit with a smell ever so slightly of her favorite perfume, Patchouli Oil has been waiting for her to wear for a year. Sally-Sue still fits into it, a little bit snug though as it's been a year of starches; potatoes, breads and macaroni. The correctional officer shakes her head as she hands Sally-Sue her thong sandals.

"Sally-Sue, would you like to wear a pair of state shoes. There's about a foot of snow, so I don't think that your sandals are going to be able to get you where you're going with your toes freezing."

"Do I need to pay for them?"

"Well, you have earned about two hundred from scrubbing the kitchen floor and cleaning toilets so the shoes will cost you fifty."

"You know. This is really a rip off. First of all, I shouldn't have spent a year of my life in this joint to begin with. I'm innocent...framed...was screwed."

"Sally-Sue, I'm not here to debate with you the unfairness of life and our legal system. You either want a pair of state shoes or leave with your thong sandals. I don't really care one way or another."

"I'll pass, freeze my toes off and sue the state." The door clicks open as Sally-Sue walks through. "Goodbye and I hope to never see this place again."

Sally-Sue's relieved to get this behind her. She scans the waiting room and sees Juney Bea sitting in a corner. Juney Bea's aged. She's thin, her curly hair looks like an out grown perm and her clothing is wrinkled and loose. Sally-Sue walks over as Juney Bea stands up, with her arms extended. She meets her girlfriend mid-way. They hug.

"Well, Sally-Sue it's so good to see you."

"Juney Bea, let's get the hell out of this hole."

The two Virginia Tech friends make a hasty exit. As Sally-Sue opens freedom's door the bright sun mingled with a foot of snow is blinding. Her toes hit the snow and shock her system. They arrive at Juney Bea's blue Ford, open the doors and plop inside. Sally-Sue rolls her window down, extends her right arm outside the window and extends her middle finger, pointing it up to the sky, however; aiming for the jail as Juney Bea cranks the engine.

Chip Wells is sitting at his desk reviewing eligibility redeterminations when he hears a knock at the front door. He shuffles over to the door with Sergeant and Bella at his heels. Their tails are wagging so they must know who is there. He looks out the window and Jane and Jon are at the door with wide smiles on their faces. Chip unlocks the door.

"Hey guys, what's up? I see you survived the blizzard."

Jane's holding a couple of cups of coffee and Jon has a Sugarbaker's bag, most likely doughnuts. They take seats in the waiting room.

"Chip, we just wanted to spend a few minutes with you. Here's a cup of coffee and we brought you some cream doughnuts."

Chip opens the bag and gets a sugar filled creamed doughnut and takes a sip of coffee.

"How are you and how's Francie?"

"Oh. I'm fine. I'm feeling kind-of overwhelmed right now with this snow and all of the paperwork or I guess I should say computer work that is due, so I decided to come to work even though State offices are closed. Francie's in the field if you're looking for her. She had a couple of reports to go out on from yesterday, so Deputy Franks is driving her around. She left me in charge of the dogs, which is no problem as they sleep all day."

"Did you hear about the abandoned foals?" Jon interjects.

"Yes. Kaylee and I were talking about it yesterday after Francie called Kaylee to inform her. Francie was pretty upset that somebody would do that."

"That's why we're here. We're concerned about Francie getting really upset about this. Her mom was supposed to come yesterday from Charlottesville, but didn't arrive probably because of the storm." Jane looks at Jon, takes a sip of coffee and begins to pet Bella. "She had a really rough go of it last year when this guy tried to kill Trooper and her. We promised her mother, that we would keep an eye on Francie."

Chip takes another sip of coffee and finishes his cream doughnut. He smiles and looks down at Sergeant who's sitting in front of Jon, getting petted. "I think that she's OK. I'll let you know if there is anything wrong.

"Chip, how about if we take Sergeant and Bella for a couple of hours. We've decided to have story time today since schools are closed."

"That's perfect, Jane. Thanks for asking. I know that the kids as well as the dogs enjoy story time. Francie enjoys listening to you read too."

Jane and Jon stand, the dogs jump on Jon anticipating leaving as Chip holds the door and everybody vacates. The wind blows snow onto Chip's face. In the distance he hears a sea gull screech as three ducks wobble across Main Street.

Juney Bea and Sally-Sue are traveling East on I-64. They've just passed Richmond; travel is extremely slow due to the unplowed roads and Sally-Sue's antsy. This traffic congestion is getting on her nerves. She's in a crap mood between snow, traffic and Juney Bea singing an old Carole King song, *Smackwater Jack.*

"Now Smackwater Jack he bought a shot gun, 'cause he was in the mood for a little confrontation. He just a- let it all hang loose, he didn't think about the noose, he couldn't take no more abuse, so he shot down the congregation."

Of course, Juney Bea adds a different flavor to the song; "Now Sally-Sue Moon's bought a shot gun, 'cause she was in the mood for a little confrontation. She's gonna let Batista's know, she couldn't take no more abuse, so she shot down social service. Yeah, you can't talk to a Moon, with a jar full of dank…yeah, yeah…so she shot…social service."

Sally-Sue's trying hard to ignore her best friend. It's been a tough year for both. Better not stir the pot. Sally-Sue looks out of the side mirror. They've just passed Richmond. The sky line of tall buildings and VCU Medical Center is outlined.

Juney Bea takes the Laburnum Avenue exit and decides to eat lunch at Applebee's. She parks. The mismatched pair shuffle inside and sit in a booth by a window facing Laburnum. With elbows on the table, Juney Bea holds her head in her hands as Sally-Sue's biting her finger nail.

While waiting for a waitress, Juney Bea elicits conversation as neither has said much.

"So Sally-Sue, how are you really doing?"

"Not good Juney Bea. I'd like to thank you for driving from New York City and for really being there for me. This has been a year from hell. One thing I can say about spending a year behind bars is that I have had a year to think about how I was set-up. I think that it was either Gertrude and or her worthless shit for a daughter, Francie. One of them is a pothead or both.

"I know. We took the hit. We lost our jobs. I know that I look as bad as I feel. It hasn't been easy trying to sell used clothing in Manhattan. My career in social work is ruined. I can't even get hired in New York."

The waitress comes and orders are taken. Sweet tea, eggs, once over with grits. "I will never be able to make the money that I was selling bargain basement garments. I'm no longer selling clothing located in the garment district. I am selling clothes near Times Square, in a small store where I rent a space."

The food arrives as Sally-Sue continues to listen to her friend and stare out the window. They begin to eat, each drinking sweet tea first. "They don't make sweet tea in New York. Those northerners put a package of sugar in their cold tea. It doesn't make sense. The sugar doesn't melt, goes to the bottom, and they stir their tea periodically, I guess hoping that the sugar will melt. It tastes like shit."

"Juney Bea, quit complaining. Try eating jail house food and Kool-Aid for a year."

"I'm sorry. I need to be more sensitive. You would think as an ex-social worker that I would be more understanding. I've basically thrown philosophy out the door. Life's a crock...in reality; it's every man for their self."

"Boy, Juney Bea, I thought that my ideals had changed in a year. You're really bitter."

Sally-Sue smothers her grits with butter and mixes her eggs with a little ketchup as Juney Bea enjoys the rest of her sweet tea. The outside American flag's flapping with the cold northern breeze as freshly fallen snows glistening in the sun light. Both chow down, take bathroom breaks, pay their bills and return to

Juney Bea's beat up Ford. Juney Bea pulls out and proceeds toward Richmond International Airport.

"I want to drive east for a bit through Sandston. I like this little community. Some of the Civil War was fought here."

"I think that the battle fought was called, the Battle of Seven Pines. The Yanks came without sweet tea and tried to claim the victory."

"Sally-Sue, I have missed your sense of humor this past year. Maybe I might consider relocating since your returning home."

"I'm really looking forward to living at home and sleeping in my own bed. You are spending a few days aren't you?"

"Sounds good to me. I've really missed seafood, especially Bill's broiled flounder."

"Me too. You need to cheer up Sally-Sue. Shit happens and it happened to us."

"Just wondering, do you know if Chief Winston ever retired?"

"Yes, he did, after you were in court. I was flipping the television channels and caught a segment of *60 Minutes*. The Chief and that state police guy, Ben Benson were interviewed about Bart Connors, who's synonymous as the Eastern Shore Wind Chime Killer. The Chief went out in glory. We went out as turds."

"I know. I'm going to find out who's in charge, make an appointment and make it a point to request that an investigation commence as to whose the pothead that put the weed beneath Twinkies in Wanda Burton's Biscotti jar."

"Sally-Sue I think you need to let *sleeping dogs lie* as the saying goes."

"I know that I should, however; I'm not going to."

14

Chip Wells, is tired of facing his computer and working-up food stamp applications and Medicaid. He has a stack of redeterminations due so that clients can continue to receive their benefits. Given the economic conditions there's been an abrupt surge in need of food stamps and he's having difficulty keeping up.

Chip takes a sip of water, glances at his watch and decides to give Kaylee a visit at her antique shop at the mall. Francie's dogs are with Jane and Jon so he doesn't have to be concerned that they will become bored and eat the agency. Bella loves paper and will consume your documentation if left on the floor or within muzzle reach. Francie has a habit of leaving case records on her office floor and Bella's forever eating notes, and narratives.

Chip turns off his computer, pushes his chair back, and stands. He walks into the kitchen and takes a look at the park. The day's gorgeous, bright and sunny. Ducks are slowly waddling around, although having a difficult time, due to the height of the snow. Drifts are present along the dock and boats are covered with snow and ice. A couple of local fishermen are on deck, shoveling icy snow from one of the deep sea fishing boats. The one fisherman shakes his head in unison as he throws snow overboard.

Chip locks the agency door, crosses Main and enters the mall. Kaylee's in her shop, with her back to the door, staring at the computer. A couple of kittens are running up the stairs to the second floor.

She glances up and turns when she hears footsteps. "Hey Chip, what a pleasant surprise!"

"I got bored at work and thought I'd take a walk and see if you wanted to have lunch. I think the only two places opened are Bill's or Main Street Coffee Shop."

"I don't think that the coffee shop is opened. I walked by a couple of hours ago and the place is dark and no one's shoveled."

"OK. How about Bill's?"

"Alright. Quick question. What do you know about the four abandoned foals?"

"Not much. I just heard that the four were found half frozen at the Corral Pen in Assateague"

"I spoke with Francie late last night. She's been playing around on the computer entering abandoned foals; foals born late in the season and thinks she may have a theory. She didn't want to tell me over the phone, so she's supposed to swing by later to see me."

"Um...I might hang around to hear her theory. You know, Francie's incredible with her common sense intelligence. She's really good at figuring stuff out, especially child abuse cases. That's what really makes her first-rate at investigations. She gets the job completed quickly... fast assessments as she's able to figure out family systems swiftly and has such good ability to understand the *writing on the wall.*" Paul, our supervisor, uses Francie as an example as she's always current on narratives, fixes the problem and closes her cases in a timely manner. Others keep cases opened for years, aren't current on narratives and don't visit their client for months. That leads to non-compliance with policy and procedure and makes the agency look bad."

"I know. Last year she complained about Sally-Sue Moon, her supervisor and how Sally-Sue had her favorites. She looked the other way for those she liked and came down hard for those she didn't. I've known Francie for a couple of years and she's really exceptional. That's why I'm anxious to hear her theory. I do have my own theory that I want to discuss also."

"Well, I'll listen to your theories and choose which one it could be."

Jodi's sitting at her desk reading reports. In a few minutes it's muster for the night shift. Her plan is to discuss the foals and also to alert deputies that there's been an art heist. Frances Benjamin Johnston's donated photos housed in the Library of Congress have been stolen. Since many of her photos were taken on the Eastern Shore, Jodi feels it imperative to inform staff of the possibility that Ms. Johnston's photographs may turn up here. Thieves will go to where the market is...supply and demand.

Jodi hears footsteps coming down the hallway towards her office. She swings her chair around and faces the door. It's Brittany. She enters wearing sun glasses.

"Hi Brittany, what's up with the glasses."

"Jodi, can I speak with you privately."

Jodi shifts in her chair and looks up through her bangs. "Sure thing...is there something wrong?"

Brittany walks in, "Yeah, there's a lot wrong." She sits and puts her face into her hands and looks down. She removes her glasses and she's sporting a large black right eye."

Jodi gets up out of her chair and walks over to where Brittany's sitting. Brittany begins to sob.

"Brittany, what's happened?"

"It's Mike. He did this to me. I caught up with him yesterday near Watts Estates. I left work early due to the snow and met him near Wallops at the Fast Mart. He had just left Elizabeth Allen's place. He was in a bad mood. A big rush as he said that he was on his way to Temperanceville. I asked him what was going on. We were sitting in my car. He was sitting in the passenger seat...said it wasn't my business. He told me to shut the fuck up and then punched me in the eye, got out of my car, slamming the door. He got into his truck; shot me the bird as he turned his truck onto Route 13, heading for Temperanceville. I sat there in shock. I'm still in shock. I think he has something to do with those foals. It's just a hunch."

"Well, Brittany. I am so sorry that this happened to you. Have you made an appointment to get your eye checked?"

"No. I'm so embarrassed. I couldn't go to Dr. Smith. He's on the island and knows everybody including my parents. I don't want anybody to know about this. I don't want to do a police report. I'm going to break up with him. I just want this ugly event to go away."

"Brittany, I don't think that it can go away. I'm captain and it's against the law what he did. He assaulted you. This comes under domestic violence. You don't need to be the reporter."

"Don't you think I know all of this Jodi? I don't want anybody knowing. It will be all over the island what he's done. I just want it to go away.

"Explain to me about your hunch."

"A couple of months ago, he had a wad of cash in his pocket. He paid cash for this now worthless diamond."

Jodi walks back to her desk. She really doesn't think that the diamond's worthless only the man that purchased it.

"Well, he said that his brother, Marty, you do know that he has an identical twin?"

"No, I didn't. Where does Marty live?"

"He's a life guard during the summer in Atlantic City and during the winter he's a guard in Miami."

"I didn't know that. Where are Mike and Marty from?"

"They were basically raised on the island as we attended school together from about third grade on." Brittany attempts a smile, looks down at her diamond, and nods her head. A tear drips onto her dress. She brings her head and eyes back to Jodi, looking her squarely in the eye. "Mike said that his brother, Marty was involved with something big and since his brother wasn't living here had asked Mike to oversee operations. Mike said that he was making about five-hundred per week, and it had to do with horses."

"Did he say exactly where this operation was occurring?"

"No, I haven't a clue."

Warren McKinney's been driving around Temperanceville reciting the message that Park Ranger Molly Smith had attached to her door. *Temperanceville foals began, Pony Corral's their end...Hurry, Park Ranger, Danger.* Warren's driving up and down back roads looking for four mares. With the snow and drifts Warren has almost gotten his vehicle stuck a couple of times. He's had to stop as one tire is flat and he's exhausted. Between the snow and this investigation it's taxing. He changes the tire and heads for Conquest Chapel. As he's passing Conquest Chapel he spots Deputy Greg Franks and Francie Batista driving by. He flags Greg Franks to stop.

"Hey, Warren. What are you doing here?"

Francie puts the passenger window down to hear their conversation.

"Well, I'm driving around because Molly had a message attached to her door yesterday. It said, Temperanceville foals began, Pony Corral's their end...Hurry, Park Ranger, Danger."

"Is that how she found the foals?"

"No. She found the note after she returned from the park. I think that the person who put the note there knew about the foals and wanted them found before they froze to death, however; didn't know that Molly was already at work."

"So, Warren, you're driving around looking for mares?"

"Yeah. If I see any, I'm going to stop at the farm and ask some questions. Foals normally aren't born in winter. This is really strange."

Francie's taking in the conversation. *If I were doing something illegal, I wouldn't have the mares outside. I would have them in a barn somewhere.*

"Well, Francie and I are on our way to interview an elderly woman who lives near T's Corner. We'll keep in mind what you said and call you if we see anything strange."

"OK. Thanks. I'm heading back to Chincoteague. I'm going to speak with Captain Burgess about the note and ask that some deputies start driving around Temperanceville."

"Alright. We'll give you a call if anything is out of place."

15

We continue to T's Corner. "You know Greg; I wouldn't be looking outside like Warren's doing if I had four mares that just gave birth. I would have them in a barn. What this person did is criminal and I don't think that he or she for that matter would blatantly have mares outside for folks to see."

"Well, you may be right. Let's see if we find anything out of the ordinary out this way while we're visiting, what's the person's name?"

"Relax Greg, when I tell you this. The person that we are visiting for me to interview is an elderly woman named, Carrie Sadie Nation-Savage."

"Who?"

"Ms. Nation-Savage was named after two women. Cary Nation traveled around preaching about the evils of drinking and that other woman, Sadie Savage agreed. They connected at one point both believing in the Temperance movement."

"Wasn't that about the evils of drinking?"

"Yep, yep...that's how Temperanceville got its name. No liquor or barrooms."

"So, what's up with the interview?"

"You'll have to wait and see. I don't want to spoil your fun this afternoon."

Greg makes a couple of turns and goes down a snowy road. The mailbox has Nation-Savage on it. "This is it, Greg." I giggle and reach for a sip from my bottled water.

Greg picks up the radio and calls dispatch, informing of his whereabouts.

I open the car door and swing my legs onto the snowy ground. My mucking boots have remained cold and damp. I grab my notebook and adult protective service report. Greg follows me to the front door. We slide a few times as we reach the door. It's difficult to decipher where the steps are, as no one has shoveled. I give a stiff knock. As I'm about to knock again, Abby Soloman opens the door. *My damn luck. I hate it when the reporter's present during an interview...very uncomfortable.*

"Oh, hi Abby. I didn't think that you were going to be here today. I'm sorry that I didn't get the chance to interview your grandmother yesterday, but the weather was nasty."

"It's OK. I decided to spend a couple of days with my grandmother. Please come in and who are you with?"

"Yes, this is Deputy Greg Franks. The only reason that he's with me is that I can't drive the county car in all of this snow. I don't usually complete interviews with him."

"Well, it's a pleasure to meet you, please come in. My grandmother is sitting and rocking in her favorite chair by the living room window enjoying the snowy scenery."

"After introductions Abby, I will need to interview your grandmother alone."

"Thanks fine." We continue walking and reach the living room where Carry Sadie Nation-Savage, is sitting...rocking away the day.

"Grandmother, you have company today."

I walk over to the rocking chair where Ms. Nation-Savage is sitting. Greg's behind me. Ms. Nation-Savage is smiling.

"Please take a seat. Would you like hot tea?"

"No thank you ma'am."

"My... it's such a cold wintery day. It's nice to watch the birds eating from the feeders and look at all of this snow! I love snow. It reminds me of my youth when I would sleigh ride. We had a horse name Millie, which pulled my father's plow. When we had snow, Pa would hook-up Millie to a sleigh and we would travel around the farm. And what a treat that was?"

"That's a really wonderful memory, ma'am." I glance at Abby as she leaves the living room. Greg's standing at the window studying birds. I decide to sit on the sofa, next to Ms. Nation-Savage. I make myself comfortable and clear my throat. "Ms. Nation-Savage, I'm a social worker and my name is Francie Batista. This is Greg Franks. He's with the sheriff's department and is driving me around today due to the condition of roads."

"And what does a social worker want with me?"

"Somebody who cares about you contacted me and wanted me to visit with you."

"Why would someone send you here?"

"Well, I work with individuals who may be abused, neglected or someone's stealing their money."

"Nobody's stealing my money…I have it in the bank up the street."

"That's really good ma'am. I was afraid that you were going to tell me that you had it stuffed under your mattress."

Ms. Nation-Savage gives out a hearty laugh and taps the palm of her hand on her knee. The rocking chairs moving…back and forth…back and forth and Greg's shaking his head…back and forth…back and forth.

"Anyway, today is considered as a wellness check. I'd like to ask you a few questions and see how you are, if I may ma'am?"

"Of course you may. Officer, isn't she as cute as she can be?"

Greg's taken off guard, smiles and continues to look outside.

"OK, Ms. Nation-Savage I'd like to begin our interview. How are you?"

"I'm fine."

"I know that you live by yourself. Do you have anyone helping you keep your house so neat and clean? And I can smell something good baking in the oven. Do you cook for yourself?"

"Ms. Batista, I'm able to cook and I clean the house. I run the vacuum once a week, get down on my hands and knees and clean my kitchen and bathroom floors. I still drive and drive to food stores and to church."

"I can tell by looking around how clean and tidy your home is."

"How long have you lived here, ma'am?"

"I've lived here all of my life. This is my parents' farm. It's no longer a farm, sold acres throughout the years, but it's mine and I plan to live here until my last breath."

"So how old are you Ms. Nation-Savage."

"I was born in 1945 and just had a birthday. I'm 65 and not considered old, after all I'm a Baby Boomer. I've been drawing social security for a couple of months. I keep in shape by gardening, walking and joined Gold Gym a few weeks ago. I'm pumping weights. I really don't understand why somebody is concerned about me."

"Let me ask you a few more questions ma'am and then I will leave. You seem fine to me, but I still need to make sure."

Greg shifts his weight. He knows that I'm about to get down to the nitty-gritty of the report.

"What I'd like to do is to discuss the nature of this report with you."

"That is fine with me, Ms. Batista."

"Ms. Nation-Savage, the reporter says that lately you've been talking about a gentleman by the name of Ron Jeremy. Prior to coming I had a few minutes to Google Ron Jeremy on the computer and if it's the same Ron Jeremy that you've been speaking of, he is a porn star." I divert my eyes and glace across the room at Greg, who's changed how he's standing and is staring at Ms. Nation-Savage.

"Ms. Batista, is that what this is about?"

"Yes it is."

"Do you know Ron Jeremy, the porn star?"

"Sure do. I know him well missy."

"Oh? So it is true that you were an extra in a movie that Ron Jeremy starred in?"

"Yes, and I know where this conversation is going."

I angle my body so that I'm closer to Ms. Nation-Savage and I notice that the shuffling in the kitchen has stopped. Obviously, Abby has stopped puttering and is intent on listening.

"Ms. Batista, I'm a religious woman, but I will let you in on a little secret. It was around 1979, I was in my thirties visiting my first cousin, Louise in New York. She's dead now, but we had the summer of our lives. Ron Jeremy was just getting started. I think that he was a teacher somewhere in upstate New York. Anyway, he quit teaching, didn't feel fulfilled. As you know Ron's known for his willy thus became a porno star."

I smile and sit straight up on the sofa ready to hear the climax. Greg decides to walk across the living room and take a seat next to me. He is looking interested in this conversation.

"Ron needed extras for one of his movies and he advertised in the *New York Times* for the movie, *Bloody Bible Camp*. Louise and I tried out. We were hired to play the part of Christian counselors. Louise and I had the time of our lives...we had smiles on our faces and made many friends. It was the best summer of my life! Louise felt the same way. And when the movie was released we drove to Richmond, and watched it at the Biograph Theater."

I smile and hear glass hit the kitchen floor…Ms. Nation-Savage continues…who in their right mind would interrupt…Greg sure as hell isn't…as I'm thinking of finding a copy of this movie.

"I've never seen a willy like it before. Ron saw me looking during one of his scenes and says to me, "Its home grown Cary." *God, I do need a bong hit and she aint talkin' pot.* "You do know what I'm aiming at, Ms. Batista." Ms. Nation-Savage throws her head back with hearty laughing and the rocking chair almost falls totally over. Greg springs into action moving with purpose to steady the rocking as he holds his hands on the back of Ms. Nation-Savage's rocking chair. I'm grinning from ear to ear. My eyes are tearing, so I use my gloves to wipe them.

"Well, for once in my life, I'm lost for words, Ms. Nation-Savage. I'm delighted that you had a wonderful experience at summer camp and have shared with me what you did on your summer vacation." I laugh at my humor as Ms. Nation-Savage turns in her chair facing the kitchen.

"Abby, dear, come into this room. I know that you've been listening. I know that you're the person that wanted Ms. Batista to interview me."

Abby enters the living room with her head down. "Why didn't you ask me dear? Are you embarrassed?"

"Grandmother, I was worried that you had mental health problems. You've just started talking about Ron Jeremy. I thought that you were getting Alzheimer's. I just can't imagine you in a movie with Ron Jeremy."

"When we are young we have adventures. Louise and I needed to let our hair down and have some good fun, something of which I couldn't do living in Temperanceville, especially with this name. Can you imagine what gossip would have generated if I ever drank, smoked pot and fornicated in the back seat of a car around here?"

"Grandmother!"

"Abby, you're like an old prune! Of course, I smoked pot in the sixties, seventies, and maybe once or twice in the eighties. I'd do it now if I could find some." *I can see where this conversation is heading and it isn't the "Bridge to Nowhere."*

I clear my throat, stand up and stand in front of Ms. Nation-Savage. I kneel along side of her and we spend a moment looking at the birds, which are enjoying sunflower seeds and corn. In the distance I see a lone barn.

"Ms. Nation-Savage, I can see a barn in the distance. Do you know who owns that parcel of land with the barn?"

"We sold that parcel back in 1999 to Mary and Joseph Rigatoni. They're from New Jersey and come down summers."

"Thanks so much for this information. Oh, have you seen anything of interest from over there?"

"No dear. Why would you inquire?"

"Well, Ms. Nation-Savage, if you could do me a favor? I'm looking to rent a stall in a barn for my horse; Trooper and was just wondering if you happen to see anybody over there to give me a call."

"I will let you know if I see anybody."

"Also ma'am, you are fine and healthy. Here's my card, just in case you need to get in touch with me. It has certainly been my pleasure to have met you."

"I've enjoyed your visit. Come by and visit me again sometime."

"I promise that the next time I'm out in this direction, I will give you a holler."

"Abby please see Deputy Franks and Ms. Batista to the door."

Abby walks us to the front door. She's looking embarrassed and may be lost for words.

"I'm so sorry Francie for dragging you out here."

"It's no problem. Your grandmother's fine and now you know that she was a camp counselor one summer." Greg shakes his head at that low blow. I smile and begin the decent to the vehicle.

Abby shuts the door as we grope down front steps with slight smiles on our faces. Greg opens the passenger door and I fold in, slumping onto the seat, bursting into laughter.

Greg opens his door, cranks the engine and when he's down the driveway heading towards Chincoteague lets out the loudest hoot that I've ever heard.

"Abby's probably getting reamed by grandma for that one!" Greg says thumping his thumbs onto the steering wheel. He's playing drums to his own beat.

"I know. I went on the internet and looked up Ron Jeremy. It fits especially if she was up in New York. And did you hear the name of the folks from New Jersey, Mary and Joseph Rigatoni. What is it with folks from New Jersey? I mean at times I'm embarrassed to be Italian."

"Are you talking about *Jersey Shore* the hit reality show as I can't say that I've seen it?"

"I am partially, but really talking about the last name of Rigatoni...pasta. What a last name."

"Don't we have two *Jersey Shore* transplants living on Chincoteague Island? Let me see, Luciano Levine, a Jewish-Italian guy, who sings at the Village Restaurant."

"Yep...yep. He's the guy who volunteers with the fire department and was out at the fairgrounds mucking horse stalls when he found the dead Chincoteague pony last year when the killer was loose."

"Yeah, you're right."

"And Luciano married his Guidette girlfriend, Maria-Frances DeFore. He purchased his first horse about one year ago and his dream has come true. He's a Salt Water Cowboy. I see them at church on Sundays and Holy Days. They look very happy."

"Chincoteague is becoming the melting pot for assimilation."

"I wonder how many true islanders are living in Chincoteague. You know, from families that founded the place...this has been all too much of a day...Ron Jeremy and Jersey Shore Guidos."

Greg's smiling and tapping his fingers on the steering wheel. We're heading back to Chincoteague. I'm deep in thought. My plan is to return to the agency, get on the computer and speak with Kaylee.

Driving along I'm deep in thought. I'm going to go back to the agency and look something up on the computer. I think I know what's happening in Temperanceville, however; don't want to say anything to Greg. That's all I need is him trailing behind me when what I plan to do has a degree of trespassing, and maybe breaking and entering.

Driving over the new bridge, Chincoteague looks intriguing. There's snow and icy patches on top of the bay. Ripples of snow and ice are frozen, appearing as ice sculptures.

"Greg, if you could drop me at the agency I'd appreciate it. I have a few more tasks to do before calling it a day. I think that it's going to be a cold one once the sun goes down. This snow isn't going to go anywhere."

"You got that right. Do you need me to drive you anywhere tomorrow?"

"I don't think so Greg. I'll look at new reports and call you if I need to travel away from the island. Chincoteague streets look fine, thanks to Sammy."

Greg and I say goodbye and as I unlock the agency's front door, it feels like a ghost town. The lights are out and the dogs don't greet me at the door. Chip's posted a note on his desk explaining that he's over at Kaylee's store and that Sergeant and Bella are with Jane and Jon. I exhale a breath of relief and walk to my office. I turn on my office light, walk to my desk and boot my computer. My mind's on the foals. I Google the Friends of Animals site that I read while in college. I'd bet my job those foals are PMU babies.

"Yes!" I leap from my seat, make a dash through the agency, cross Main, open the door of the mall and sprint to Kaylee's store. I find, Kaylee and Chip sitting side by side, appearing deep in conversation. As I enter, they jump.

"Hey guys. I have a theory and need you to come with me."

"Is your theory about the foals?

"Yep, yep and if my theory is correct, I know where the mares are."

"I have a theory too, Kaylee says as she reaches for her computer print-out."

I glance down. "Kaylee we're thinking on the same level."

"Chip, you have a 4-wheel drive jeep don't you?"

"Yes, and I will drive both of you wherever you desire."

16

We pile into Chip's Wrangler, go over the new bridge and head to Temperanceville. We're heading towards T's Corner nearing Conquest Chapel and there's a small road. Chip makes a left when he sees my hand go up and we follow what appears to be an icy snowy dirt road. There's a rustic log house on the right with no cars or tire tracks leading to the house. We continue past the house and a barn is visible to the left. Chip stops and parks as there are no cars around. Kaylee and I quickly exit the vehicle and head straight for the barn as Chip follows. We slide the barn door open. The stench of manure is enough to take my breath away. I turn lights on as my heart is racing and I look at Kaylee, who's pale and has placed her hand over her nose. Chip's standing next to Kaylee looking shocked.

"Guys, this is a PMU farm..."The pill that kills"...look at these poor mares, standing in days of manure, tied in livestock stalls without food and water." Tears form in my eyes as I'm witness to this abuse and neglect.

Kaylee has brought her camera and starts to take some pictures. The mares have Urine Collection Devices to collect their urine. "Chip, lift the tail on this Draft Horse, so that I can take a look." Kaylee says following Chip to one of the stalls. He lifts the tail and Kaylee screams, "Look at the infection from urine and bacterial buildup causing numerous lesions. This is horrendous."

I'm further along the aisle and am observing a mare in tremendous stress. She's too large for the stall, can't lie down and has something wrong with her back hoof. She's strapped in the front and tied in the back. I look at the mare next to her. There's manure in her water bin, no water for her to drink and she's standing in what appears to be several day's worth of manure if not weeks. None of the mares can move more than three steps and they are unable to lie down.

"Kaylee and Chip, there must be about twenty horses here. I need you to take some pictures of this mare's infected hoof and the one next to her."

"What's this all about Kaylee? Chip says as he walks with Kaylee. What exactly is PMU? There's one pathetic horse after another in livestock stalls. All in the same degrading and disgusting conditions. Chip's looking as though he's going to vomit.

"You want to know what this shit is Chip, it's called Premarin. These mares are pregnant and are producing urine with hormones to help menopausal women not to have hot flashes. My mom was just placed on Premarin by her doctor as she's having flashes. Mom didn't know that she was taking a urine pill, from a horse."

"Did you inform her?"

"Yep...and I sent her information. I haven't spoken to her about the attachment of my e-mail yet. I'm sure that she freaked."

"Chip, the abandoned foals are PMU foals. They are usually slaughtered and sent to Japan and Europe because they offer folks delicious tender vittles. The mares that don't get pregnant are shipped to slaughter houses." Kaylee explains as she taking additional pictures.

"And for the foals that don't make it, they have usually frozen to death, as PMU farmers take the mare out to a pen for her to foal without shelter. Since some of these farms are located in the Northwest, the foals either freeze to death, starve or are transported to slaughter houses. The mares are impregnated again and the cycle continues." Kaylee starts to cry and Chip comes to her and wraps his arms around her. He kisses Kaylee on her forehead, like a mother would do, when her child is in pain.

Kaylee and I begin to look around the barn for some hay and a water faucet. "Chip and Kaylee, whoever is involved with this operation is making big bucks and as sure as I'm standing here, I know that this is a PMU farm. I'll bet a year's salary."

"Let's stop and make a call to the police and also contact Warren McKinney with animal control. He's going to have to begin an investigation." Chip says as he searches his pockets for his cell.

Chip locates his cell as we hear moaning from one of the wall stalls. "What the fuck?" Chip says as the lights go out.

Kaylee and I are shoved inside the feed room; the doors slam shut and are locked. Its pitch black and frightening and I'm about to lose it. I can't stand that closed in feeling. I grab my cell from my jean pocket, open it and note one bar. The cell goes black, dark as the feed room.

"Kaylee, do you have your cell?"

"No. I left it at my shop."

"I wonder what happened to Chip."

"He didn't sound OK. I think that we're up *shit creek without a paddle.*"

With that said, I say a prayer to Saint Anthony and while I'm at it I say a prayer to St. Francis of Assisi. After a quick Sign-of –the-Cross, I take a seat on the floor.

Sally-Sue Moon and Juney Bea Karring are travelling over the Chesapeake Bay Bridge Tunnel. This bridge connects Virginia's mainland to Virginia's Eastern Shore. The women roll down their windows; take deep breaths, breathing excitedly the cold, moist salty air. It's exhilarating. They feel like college kids again.

"Feel like smoking?"

"You can't be serious. I've just gotten out of jail for pot possession."

Juney Bea rummages through her bargain bin pocketbook feels around and locates a rolled joint. She takes it from her bag. Her lighter's on the dashboard. Juney Bea lights up.

"Oh, ease up Sally-Sue. Life's a beach."

"Yeah right. Give me a hit."

Juney Bea hands Sally-Sue the joint and she takes a long inhale. She stares at the bay and enjoys watching the glistening icy water. She takes another hit and hands it back.

"Give me your cell as I want to make an appointment with the new chief of the Chincoteague Sheriff's Department."

"You've got to be crazy. You haven't been out of jail for 24-hours and you're nuts for stirring the kettle. You were found guilty and there's no going back."

"I want revenge."

"You need to move on."

"Nope. Give me your cell."

Juney Bea takes a hit and gets her cell from her bag. She hands it to Sally-Sue.

"Do you remember the number?"

"Of course. I've called it many times, case related that is."

Sally-Sue pushes the numbers on the pad and perky Brittany answers the phone.

"Hello, Brittany? This is Sally-Sue Moon. Who's in charge now that the Chief retired?

"Jodi Burgess just started her position as Captain. I'm sure that you remember her as she conducted joint investigations with Francie Batista."

"How could I forget?" Sally-Sue replies with a smirk. She grabs the joint from Juney Bea and takes another hit.

"I'll go and get her if you can wait a minute."

"I have all the time in the world, honey." Sally-Sue says with a southern drawl.

Sally-Sue can hear shuffling of feet and Brittany's muffled voice as she takes another hit.

"Hello, Ms. Moon."

"Hi, um…is it Jodi or Captain Burgess?"

"Well, since we knew one another prior to my promotion, let's just call each other by our first names."

"OK. And let's get to the chase."

"Well, Sally-Sue what's up?"

"I'm returning to my home in Oyster and as you know I've pulled time on a bogus charge. It was never my pot in that blasted Biscotti jar. I've had over a year to think about it. Plain bull shit. I was set up."

"Sally-Sue, you were charged and had your day in court. You were found guilty. I had nothing to do with it. After all you were in possession of a Biscotti jar laced with Twinkies and pot."

"You know Jodi, as well as me that you're friends that pissant Francie Batista and her mother; Gertrude had something to do with the jar. Gertrude and I go back to Virginia Tech days and I know for a fact that Gertrude smoked pot in college. Maybe she never lost her desire to be in an altered state. I would say that it was one of them who put the pot in the jar. I merely took it off of Wanda Burton's desk."

"Did you ever think that it could have been Wanda's pot as it was on her desk?"

"I thought of that too. I don't think that Wanda would be stupid enough to put her own pot inside of a Biscotti jar and leave it on her desk. It doesn't fit her profile. Anyway she's been determined insane and won't be getting out of Central State."

"Sally-Sue, you stole the jar off of Burton's desk. What exactly is this call all about?"

"I want justice. My life has been ruined. I've lost my job and I want my name cleared. I want you to reopen the investigation."

Juney Bea takes another hit of her joint as she reaches the McDonald's in Cape Charles. She attempts to hand it to Sally-Sue however; Sally-Sue shakes her head and waves her hands indicating no way.

"I have better things to do with my time. I'm not opening this up. You were found guilty and have served your time. Get on with your life Sally-Sue. Good-bye."

Jodi abruptly hangs up. Sally-Sue grabs the joint from Juney Bea's hand. "That bitch, Jodi. It was a set-up; a conspiracy and you know what my take is on this shit. I will put money on it that the pot was Francie's. She has that look about her. Curly short hair and always wearing sun glasses."

"I think that you are over the edge on this Sally-Sue and you need to move on. Nothing will be accomplished by your pursuing this. You also have that pot look, whatever the hell that is in this day and age, always wearing Patchouli Oil and walking around the agency like some aged hippie."

"Juney Bea, if you weren't my life time friend, I'd de-friend you like folks do on Facebook."

"I'm just speaking the truth and you need to listen to me. Our careers are shot as social workers. Find a passion, find something, but don't go after any of the Batista's."

They arrive at Sally-Sue's "Oyster House". It's cute and the care taker, Mildred Wallace, who's the next door neighbor, appears to have taken care of things. She's shoveled a path from the driveway to the house, cleaned off the front porch and turned on the porch lights. When the women enter the house, Mildred has turned on the heat, dusted and vacuumed. There's a stack of junk mail on the kitchen table. Over one year's worth.

Juney Bea walks to the guest bedroom and sees that the bed has fresh sheets and there's a vase of fresh mums sitting on the bedside stand. Sally-Sue's impressed with her bedroom too. Mildred's made the bed using rose flowered sheets and to add to the decor a fresh vase of white roses on Sally-Sue's night stand. Sally-Sue loves antiques so the house is a mixture of old and new mixed with a combination of old and new photographs of the Eastern Shore shown in every room. Martha Stewart would smile and be proud.

"I'm going to take the longest shower in history. How about after we rest we head for Chincoteague? I want to order a Manhattan at AJ's."

"I'm in. I want to take a shower and rest my eyes. I think I have a case of snow blindness from the long drive. I'm getting a bit of a head ache."

Beth's visiting Rick. She's falling in love with him. Her perfect fit. She's as happy as she's ever been. Rick treats her like a princess, spending money, purchasing flowers and jewelry and they enjoy intimacy. The days of escort are long gone. Beth's ready to settle for marriage, children and a dog.

Beth peers towards Rick whose reading *The Washington Post.* The dining room's just been renovated and the sun's filtering through the window. Snow can be seen in the background. Rick's appearing very intent as there's a crease between his eyes. He appears as though he's fretting. As Rick's holding the paper on an angle, he suddenly jumps up.

"Jesus, Mary and Joseph, have mercy on me." He screeches as he runs into the living room.

"Rick, my God, what's the problem."

"I'll tell you what the problem is. I've been screwed. I've purchased stolen property and need to get rid of it now!"

"OK. Calm down let's talk about it. I don't know what you are talking about."

"Try reading the front page of *The Post*." Rick's pulled a photograph off of his newly painted wall. He flings the paper to Beth.

Beth reads the front page.

The heist of the century: Frances Benjamin Johnston's donated life works of the Eastern Shore from the Library of Congress. (Photo of Drummond's Mill)

"Rick, what's this have to do with you?"

Rick gets up and walks over to the liquor cabinet and pours himself a shot followed by another of straight whiskey.

"One night when you weren't working I went over to AJ's and was sitting at the bar. This guy proceeded to sit by me and we watched a football game; I can't even remember which one. I think maybe the Eagles from Philadelphia. One thing leads to another and he asked me if I liked art and photography. I told him yeah...what the heck and we walked outside to the parking lot. This dude opened his trunk and I purchased this photo, which is the exact photo on the front page of *The Washington Post*. I got it dirt cheap only two-hundred, and thought, God this is a steal."

Beth walks over to the liquor cabinet and pours herself a shot too. She walks into the kitchen and finds a bag of chips.

"Did the dude say who he is and how he acquired it?"

"Yes. Let me see he said his name was...oh God...it's on the tip of my tongue. It was Italian like a noodle."

"What do you mean like a noodle?"

"You know like pasta. He said that he was from New Jersey."

"Not another Italian from the lovely garden state. Rick, try to relax your mind. Here eat some chips, want another shot?"

Beth leaves Rick deep in thought. The guys looking like a pasty white kid from Princeton, whose just shit his pants and doesn't want his friends to know that this is his first score. Beth pours Rick another shot, returning to where Rick's sitting staring at the gristmill.

"OK, let's get thinking. I'm from New Jersey. Where in New Jersey did this guy say he was from?"

"I think Atlantic City."

"Was there anybody there with him?"

"No. He said that he was going to meet someone later. The purchasing of this photograph was quick."

"And you say that his name sounded like a noodle, let's say the names of Italian noodles. Spaghetti?"

"NO!"

"Penne?"

"No. Dear God, I got to get rid of this photograph fast."

"Um…let me think … I once went to Newark High School with this Italian low life named Rigatoni."

"That's it Beth. His name's Sal Rigatoni!"

"What! Sal's here. I used to go out with him. What an asshole."

"He has a scumbag cousin Vince Belli and after high school they left Newark and went to the shore. The jerks started a pizza business on the boardwalk of Atlantic City. It didn't do well. Then I heard that they got into hustling fake designer clothing and women's pocketbooks. They were selling goods from the trunk of Sal's car. They're small time, into horse racing and playing the numbers."

"And, you went out with him?"

"Yeah. I went to my junior prom with him and we spent half the night screwing in the back seat of his Chevy. He almost didn't graduate from high school. Sal enjoyed late night card games and sleeping in."

"Well, your ex-boyfriend sold me a hot photo and I'm getting rid of the sonofabitch tonight. And you know what I'm going to do? I'm going back to AJ's and stiff somebody else."

"Two wrongs don't make a right, Sonny."

"Don't call me Sonny...yes, your correct...two wrongs don't make a right, however tonight it will. Maybe I'll run into Rigatoni."

17

It's getting late and Jane and Jon are ready to close Sundial Books. The sun's setting and it's cold. They're ready to walk home however; Chip hasn't come for the dogs.

"Jon, didn't Chip Wells say that after he went over to the Mall to visit with Kaylee that he would come by and get the dogs if Francie hadn't returned from the field."

"I don't recall exactly what was said, but that sounds right."

"I'm going to walk over to the agency to take a look. Maybe I just didn't understand."

Jane opens the front door and Sergeant and Bella race from the store heading for the social service agency. They're running in circles, chasing each other and having lots of fun in the deep snow. Bella's flipping snow and Sergeant is running into her. Jane's cautious that she doesn't get run over.

Jane walks up to the agency's door and there's no light. The door is locked so she decides to walk across the street to the mall. The dogs follow. Jane enters walking to the last store on the left. It's dark and Kaylee's not there. She leaves with the dogs heading back to the bookstore. Jon's standing on the sidewalk.

"What's up?"

"I don't know. This is not like Francie or Chip not to pick up the dogs. Let's leave a note on the agency door saying that we have taken them home."

"I'll write the note and walk back to the agency." Jon says as he enters his store to locate a piece of paper and pen. "The dogs are full of energy so I'll take them with me. How about if you lock up, and we'll meet in front of the theater?"

Jon walks as Sergeant and Bella continue to play chase. He places a note on the agency's front door and walks in the alley between buildings letting the dogs run around the park. The night's crisp and a few ducks are sitting on the dock enjoying pieces of fish most likely from one of the fishermen. Jon calls the dogs, returns to Main, and stands in front of the theater waiting for Jane. He can see her walking from the store, crossing Main.

"Jon, I'm really worried. Perhaps I should call Jodi to see if she knows where Jon, Kaylee and Francie are?"

"I think that we should wait a few hours; perhaps Francie needed Chip in the field and Kaylee may have closed early."

Jane and Jon walk hand in hand home as a shooting star crosses overhead. Jane shivers. Sergeant and Bella are oblivious that Francie is missing.

It's freezing in the tack room and the smell of manure and urine is overpowering. Kaylee and I are cold as we didn't dress for the elements. It was just supposed to be a quick visit to this barn to check on my hunch.

"Kaylee, do you happen to have a lighter?"

"I wish I did. I don't smoke. I wonder what's happened to Chip."

"Something horrible, I fear. We need to not freeze to death and to figure a way out of this mess."

"Who do you think is making pregnant horse urine?"

"I really don't know. But whoever is running this operation didn't think about the gestational period of a horse. I don't think the person or persons involved are experienced. Perhaps this is their first time."

"I know what you are saying. I wonder how Molly, the park ranger fits into this. Maybe the person isn't as heartless as we are thinking."

"What about Molly?"

Kaylee and I inch are way to each other. We are shivering.

"When Molly returned from Assateague after the foals were found, a note was attached to her front door. It was directing her to look around Temperanceville."

"Francie, are you as cold as I?"

"On a scale of one to ten, I'm about an eight."

"My toes and hands are so cold. I'm afraid that we're stuck here for the night."

"Well, we need to stay close to each other and keep one another warm with what little body heat we have."

"I wish Chip were with us. He's always hot. He would be able to keep both of us warm." Kaylee starts to cry. "We've just started dating. I am afraid that he could be dead."

I hold Kaylee in my arms and she cries. There isn't anything that we can do about this situation. We could scream, but nobody is around to hear us. It was a stupid decision on my part not to tell Greg or Jane and Jon where we are. I'm wondering how Sergeant and Bella are?

"Kaylee, prior to getting pushed into this feed room, were you able to see anything, such as; horse blankets, saddle pads, tarps…anything that we would be able to find and cover ourselves with?"

"No. I saw bales of straw."

We get up and grope our way around. Now I know what it's like to be blind. Kaylee and I trip over a few mysterious items and Kaylee is able to make her way to a bale. I follow her voice and we fish around for the twine to break it. Flakes of straw fill the floor. We layer the floor and ourselves with straw.

The wind picks up and howls as wolves. Unsettled horses neigh. The sound of someone crying and groaning intermingles with the night's ominous sounds as Kaylee and I hug each other and weep.

Rick LaSlick is driving to AJ's for a few drinks. He can't believe that he has purchased stolen property and to top it off, this woman, Frances Benjamin Johnston was a friend of his grandmothers. He's freaking out. How can all of this interlace, especially since his mother's arrival in Virginia. Fate! Rick recalls his mother, acquiring some black and white photos of New Orleans street people and Orleans's unique architecture, after his grandmother, Marie Angelique died in 1962. Rick's mother was going through some of her mother's possessions and came upon a trunk in the attic. There among discarded vases, old family letters and photos was a letter written to his grandmother from Frances Johnston.

Rick's mother, who loves art, fell in love with the uniqueness of Ms. Johnston's photos. The letter to Marie Angelique thanked his grandmother for her southern hospitality. The photos were a present.

Rick's mother framed all of the photographs and still has them on display throughout her home. Evidently Marie Angelique and Frances Johnston sipped afternoon tea in the winter and drank sweet tea in the summer. They were avid photographers frequently traveling around New Orleans to take unique pictures of folks and old buildings. Rick surmises that Frances Benjamin Johnston must have relocated to New Orleans as she was a resident of New Orleans when she died.

This mess that he's gotten into is going to be his secret. Beth has sworn that she won't tell anybody and he believes her. She's such a good person. Rick's going to surprise her with a piece of jewelry for Christmas. He'll never mention Frances Benjamin Johnston's name to his mother.

As he's pulling into AJ's parking lot, Rick's thankful that Beth isn't working. He's feeling a little guilty about his plan, however; he doesn't see any other way. He doesn't want to burn the photo, it's worth too much. It would be a sin to destroy, and a sin to keep stolen property.

Marie Theresa LaSlick's sitting at Gertrude Batista's kitchen table with a hot cup of tea, a tad of honey and a little bit of cream reading *The Richmond Times Dispatch*. She's reading an article about the stolen photos of Frances Benjamin Johnston's from the Library of Congress.

"Gertrude, I have photos taken by Frances Johnston in my home in New Orleans. My mother and she were friends."

"Oh really?" Gertrude says in a sarcastic manner. *This woman is really demented. First she thinks I'm married to her son and now she has photographs taken by Frances Benjamin Johnston.*

"She came to New Orleans in the late 1940's and died in about 1952. My mother, Marie Angelique and Ms. Johnston were friends. They took photos together and had afternoon tea."

"That's really nice Mrs. LaSlick. Have you packed as we're leaving very early tomorrow for the Eastern Shore? We are going to meet my daughter, Francie, who's a social worker and your son, Rick to discuss your situation. I'm going to get up early tomorrow and feed the horses at about five. I plan to be on the road by six."

Mrs. LaSlick continues reading and glances up from the paper. "What situation are you speaking of?"

"Oh nothing."

It's about six in the evening and Captain Burgess is attending her first muster. She's a little nervous, not knowing everyone in the room. Sergeant Jones is in charge of the evening shift.

"We have the captain attending our muster this evening. She plans to attend periodically so that she is up on what's happening. Let's go over our evening roster."

Staff is handed a print-out of top news going on for the evening. Jodi glances at the list and notices the words, foals.

"The latest on the abandonment of the foals: According to Doug Fields, the foals are not Chincoteague ponies. He says that they were dropped off. The latest lead is that a note was found attached to the park ranger's front door, indicating that the foals came from Temperanceville."

Deputy Greg Franks interjects, "Yes, I was transporting Francie Batista, our island social worker, on field trips these past few days. We ran into Warren McKinney, our animal warden. He was out and about looking for horses in pastures. Francie mentioned to me that if she had dumped four foals, then she wouldn't have the mares on display out in a pasture, but would house them securely inside a barn. I think that we need to start asking some questions when we come across a barn and don't see any animals."

"That's a really good point. Let's be vigilant about this. We can't have every Tom, Dick or Harry, tossing foals that they don't want."

Sergeant Jones looks down and studies the second point. "Ok, who doesn't know who Frances Benjamin Johnston was?" All hands go up. "Oh, I can tell that I have a group of deputies that don't frequent museums or art shows or know Eastern Shore history."

Everybody gives a hearty laugh to Jones' humor, which is usually rather stale. "Since I didn't know before reading the paper, I'll give the floor to the Captain."

Jodi smiles and comes to the front of the room. She has put together some printouts of the stolen photographs and has them displayed on an overhead. She shows three photographs of Drummond's Mill; one is an old store, another an old cabin and last is a photo of a mill. "These are examples of what some of the photograph's look like, which were stolen recently from the Library of Congress. Ms. Johnston's work is priceless. She came to the Eastern Shore in the 1930's and took a lot of photos of structures along the shore. Ms. Johnston later donated her work to the Library of Congress. I have a hunch that some of her photos might show up here. What I don't want to be watching is *Antiques Roadshow* and see Bubba with one of her photos. I don't want you to profile… however; be on the lookout for out of state plates. Stop folks…and roadblocks work wonders."

The muster continues. "Eleanor Picks wants a deputy to drive by her house over on East Side Road. She says that kids are skateboarding in her front yard and tearing up her grass, which by the way is dirt. Of course this was before snow, sleet and hail."

Everybody snickers. "We know Ms. Picks as she's always complaining about something, especially during the week of pony swim." Deputy Wade interjects.

"James Childress says that when he walks his dog, there's a cat that chases his Doberman and he home. He wants the cat caught and taken to the pound."

Laughing continues, "And one more item…at Island Arts on Maddox, someone is leaving a photo a night of naked women at the front door when the shop is closed. Frequent drive- bys would help."

As the hours have continued with no sign of Chip or Francie; Jane and Jon are becoming alarmed. They've fed the dogs and Sergeant and Bella are sleeping comfortably with Fancy their cat. Bella's snoring like usual and Jon can't stand the thought of spending the night with a cat, and two dogs sharing their bed, especially Sergeant who growls while dreaming and a snoring Bella.

"Maybe we should call Gertrude?"

"No way. If we call anyone it will be Jodi." Jane says as she watches the news.

"Jane, when do you think we should call Jodi? Have you tried Francie's cell?"

"Yes. It goes to a message."

"How about if we eat dinner and think of what we need to do? Sometimes eating and relaxing helps with problem solving."

"Let's leave the dogs and walk to Captain Fish's Steaming Wharf. We can sit by the bay window and look at the semi-frozen water."

"Not funny. While we're eating we will come up with a plan. I'm really worried, Jon."

18

Rick LaSlick's turning into the parking lot of AJ's. The palms of his hands are sweating and he's having problems taking a deep breath. Rick needs to look relaxed, casual and together. He parks and glances in the back seat at the photo that is covered with a bed linen. He's driving an old Ford pick-up that he doesn't usually use as he wants to be discrete and not known.

Rick enters with actively shaking hands. God, he needs a good stiff one. He goes into the barroom. He hears the clinking of glasses and begins to feel at home. He stations himself at the bar in front of the television and begins to watch another football game. This feels like...déjà vous. Rick looks around scouting the scene and sees two women sitting at the end of the bar with drinks, eating peanuts. He motions to the bartender and purchases their next round. After a few minutes Rick walks over to them.

"Hi ladies. What brings you here tonight?" He's grinning from ear to ear.

"Food and mystery." Sally-Sue says as she leans nearer to Rick. "And what brings you here? By the way I assume that you're the person that bought us a round."

"Fun in the sun." Rick says in a New Jersey accent, like *Jersey Shore* dudes.

"Well, I thought that fun in the sun is saved for the summer."

Rick shifts closer to Sally-Sue and whispers, "It's fun in the sun all year round on Chincoteague Island."

"You got that right. By the way my name is Sally-Sue Moon and this is my friend, Juney Bea Karring."

"My name's Sal Rigatoni."

"You must be Italian." Sally-Sue says with fluttering eyes and a large smile.

"You're right. I'm Italian on both sides. My family's in the pizza pie business in Atlantic City."

"Well, we love Italian food and pizza. Isn't rigatoni pasta?"

"Boy your smart. Yes, I guess you could say that I'm named after a type of macaroni."

"Would you ladies like to join me for dinner?"

Sally-Sue jumps off her stool. Juney Bea rolls her eyes and follows.

"A table for three."

They walk into the dining room and Rick pulls out each chair for his ladies. Sally-Sue's mesmerized by the attention. Juney Bea studies the menu while eating delicious rolls. Another Manhattan is served prior to the main course.

"So ladies, do you live on the island?"

"Juney Bea lives in New York City and I live in a little village called Oyster. Have you ever heard of it?"

"No. I'm visiting from New Jersey for a few days. Is Oyster on the Maryland side or Virginia side?"

"It's near Cape Charles, so it's on the Virginia side, south of here. I own a small Oyster House, which is a type of house named after the area."

"So, Juney Bea, what do you do for a living?"

Juney Bea grabs another roll and places her menu on the table. "I design clothing for Macy's and help women dress for success."

Sally-Sue kicks her friend under the table as Juney Bea sips on her Manhattan.

"Well, that sounds very interesting. I love New York, especially the shows. Maybe the next time I go to New York, I'll look you up."

"That would be nice." Juney Bea says as she eyes Sally-Sue.

The waitress takes orders. Sally-Sue and Juney Bea order the most expensive dinner on the menu. Lobster mixed with crab. They devour homemade rolls and finish their drinks. Rick orders additional rolls and Manhattans. He continues to sip his beer. Rick orders some soup, keeping it simple as his stomach is in knots.

"So Sal, how long have you been in the pizza business?"

"Since birth. I came to work every day with my parents and watched my father and mother spin dough. The school bus driver picked me up from the pizzeria and dropped me off at the pizzeria." Rick says, taking a sip of beer.

Jon and Jane walk to Captain Fish's Steaming Wharf hand in hand, deep in thought. They haven't said a word since they left their house. They enter the restaurant in silence; sit at the bay window, looking at the dark, vacant bay. This isn't helping their anxiety levels.

"What are we going to do?"

"How about after dinner we walk by the social service agency? If no one is there we can walk across the street to the mall."

"Jon, we've already done that."

"Well, we haven't returned in the past couple of hours. This can be the first part of our plan."

"I'm really worried that something awful has happened to everyone."

"I'm thinking the same. Are you hungry Jane?"

"No, my stomach's too nervous to eat. Let's excuse ourselves and walk over to the agency."

The couple stands as the waitress is arriving with their water.

"I'm sorry, but Jane's had an emergency and we need to leave."

The waitress nods her head and Jane and Jon walk out of the restaurant.

"You're a typical male. I can't believe that you blamed me for our leaving the restaurant."

They walk quickly up Main and arrive at the agency. Nothing's changed. It's dark and the door is locked. Their note remains. Jane walks to the back portion of the building by way of the ally. The kitchen door is locked. There's a feral cat waiting to be fed. Jane pets the semi-friendly cat and speaks to it as one would a human. "I know that you're hungry and Francie usually feeds you. I don't have any cat food at the store. I'm really sorry."

Jane returns to the front of the agency with the black and white cat following.

"Jon, do we have any cat food at the store?"

"No."

"I'll come by tomorrow morning with some cat food."

Jane and Jon leave the agency. They cross Main and walk in front of the mall. It's black...no lights.

"Jon, let's head home and check on Sergeant and Bella." The couple walks along Main, passing the Roxy Theater and notices that a car is coming down the street. It's a beat up Ford that drives past them.

"Isn't that Sally-Sue sitting in the passenger seat with Juney Bea driving?" Jane asks turning around and staring as the car heads towards the new bridge.

"I didn't notice. I was looking down."

"I wonder when Sally-Sue got out of jail and what the heck she's doing on Chincoteague."

"Maybe it wasn't Sally-Sue and Juney Bea. The car passed quickly."

"I know what I saw and I saw Sally-Sue and her friend, Juney Bea. I wonder if Francie knows that they're here."

Rick's scored. His adrenaline's pumping. After paying the bill he escorts the ladies to the parking lot and holds Sally-Sue's hand. Rick whispers that he has a gift for her in his car.

"I have had a pleasant evening. I'm hopeful that our paths will cross maybe in New Jersey or New York or for that matter the next time I come to the shore."

Rick walks to his truck and opens the back door. "Juney-Bea the next time I visit Manhattan, I'll look you up at Macy's and maybe we can have dinner in Little Italy. I know a really charming small restaurant with authentic Italian cuisine."

"That would be wonderful." As Juney Bea extends her hand, Rick places a kiss on it."

"Thanks Sal for the wonderful evening and dinner. I really enjoyed myself."

"No problem. I liked the time also."

Sally-Sue's still holding Sal's left hand. She has a death grip on it. It's been awhile since a man has paid any attention to her.

"And Sally-Sue, I have a small gift for your Oyster House. I hope that it will fit with your décor."

Rick uncovers the photo and immediately, Sally-Sue's in love with it. It's a black and white photo of an old mill. She envisions framing it and hanging it to the left of her fireplace. There's an antique rocking chair in the corner and the picture will look perfect. She gives Sal a kiss on the cheek and slips him her cell number.

"Well Sal, we certainly want to thank you for the wonderful evening."

"You're welcome. Maybe we can have dinner again before I return to New Jersey. I'll give you a call tomorrow."

"That's fine." Sally-Sue replies with a twinkle in her eyes.

Rick waits for the ladies to leave. Juney-Bea's driving and Sally-Sue's holding the photo with a big smile on her face. They drive on Maddox and decide to travel "down the island." They find themselves at the Curtis Merritt Harbor, enjoying the brisk evening. Juney Bea parks and they walk the dock admiring boats. They continue, between two dunes at the end of the island.

"Isn't this where that vagrant Lucky Lou Mann lived last year?"

"He certainly had the best spot on the island, Sally-Sue."

"I wonder what ever happened to him after he was shot."

"It turns out; Wanda Burton is his niece and that Wanda's mother's Pat, who's your ex-roommate from Virginia Tech, is his sister and was our friend. Remember, we gave Wanda the job as an eligibility worker and that's one of the reasons that I got axed. I should never have listened to you Sally-Sue and hired her. She wasn't qualified and half the time didn't show for work."

"Now I'm remembering all of the drama, Juney Bea and I'm sorry that you lost your job because of me."

"Well, it is over and done with. Did you know that Wanda's a full-time resident of Central State, and Pat and Lou are taking care of their long lost relative, sweet Aunt Margie? They're related to Bart Connors now known as the Eastern Shore Wind Chime Killer. Remember, Bart's father, George was Pat and

Lou's first cousin, which makes Bart their second cousin. They never knew that their father had a brother."

The two long time friends continue walking enjoying their evening. They view lights of the mainland and are touched by the uniqueness of the moon, although a sliver, the moon is surrounded by stars.

"What a nice guy Sal Rigatoni is?"

"Well, Sally-Sue you certainly came on to the guy."

"Of course. He's good looking and I haven't gotten it since before I was locked up. I love hot Italian men and he certainly fits the profile."

"Just watch yourself. Don't you think that it was a little strange that he picked us up at the bar, bought us dinner and gave you a picture?"

"I think that he likes me and that you're jealous."

"You are delusional. I just think that it's pretty weird. And after living in New York for over a year, I don't think that he is from New Jersey. A few times his speech had a southern slur."

"I don't think so. He sounded like those guys on the *Jersey Shore* to me. Anyway, I love the photo, its real Eastern Shore looking."

Juney Bea and Sally-Sue find themselves standing in front of Juney Bea's car. The friends get in and proceed north along Main Street. They're heading for the new bridge. It's been a long day and both desire closure. "Hey, isn't that Jon and Jane from Sundial Books standing in front of the theater?

"Just go by, don't look and don't wave. I don't want them to know that I'm back. They'll tell Francie who will tell her mother."

As they're driving by the social service agency, Sally-Sue rolls the window and shoots the bird for the second time today.

"That's for you Francie and your bitch for a mother."

"Sally-Sue you've had too much to drink."

"So have you Juney Bea. How many Manhattan's did you have?"

"A few too many but nobody's on the road. We'll be fine. It's the dead of winter and Chincoteague's a ghost town.

There's a light at Maddox and Main. Juney-Bea's not paying attention and runs through it.

"Juney Bea, you've just run a red light."

"So what. Who cares? There's nobody around."

Sally-Sue looks in her side passenger mirror and sees blue lights. "I think that's a deputy who's just turned on his lights…just be cool."

"You've got to be kidding. Where's your license and registration."

"It's in the glove compartment, the registration, that is. My license is in the trunk in my purse."

Juney Bea stops the car and rolls the window down. "What's the problem sir?"

"You ran a red light. License and registration please."

"Officer my pocketbook is in the trunk of my car." Juney Bea snatches the registration from Sally-Sue's finger tips. "And here's my registration."

Juney-Bea steps out of the car. She falls down, tripping on a rock, twisting her ankle." The deputy helps her up and she walks towards the trunk and slips on some black ice. He catches her.

"Ma'am, have you been drinking?"

"I just had a couple of drinks at AJ's."

"Ma'am, you will need to take a breathalyzer."

"Sir, I am fine."

The deputy calls for back-up. His partner's a few blocks away and arrives within minutes. This deputy stands at the passenger side of the car.

"Ma'am please step out of the vehicle."

Sally-Sue can't believe that this shit is happening. She awkwardly gets out still holding her newly acquired present.

"What is in your hand, Ma'am?"

"It's just a black and white photo that I received as a present."

The officer turns on his flash light. "May I look at it?"

Sally-Sue hands the deputy the photo. He takes a look, and places the photo on the roof of the car. "Ma'am place your hands on the roof of the car, spread your legs."

"What the heck is this all about deputy?"

"You are under arrest for stolen property. You have the right to remain silent...."

"What...you can't be serious. Juney Bea?"

Sally-Sue's handcuffed and looks over the car at Juney Bea whose blowing into a tube. Within moments Juney Bea's handcuffed. They're placed in separate squad cars. *This can't be happening...what a nightmare...I've just gotten out of jail for pot possession.*

19

Jodi Burgess is asleep. She hears her cell beeping. It's on her nightstand. A text message: One photograph recovered. Two women arrested. She quickly dresses and heads to work to ascertain whose being booked.

Sally-Sue and Juney Bea remain sitting in the back of squad cars when they see Sal Rigatoni drive past. He smiles, waves and speeds by.

"Excuse me sir, excuse me deputy... the person that gave me the photo just drove past us and waved. Did you see the truck?"

"No ma'am."

Juney Bea gives Sally-Sue a look to kill from her window. "Excuse me sir, did you happen to see the gentleman that just drove past us? He's the one that gave Sally-Sue the photo."

"Tell it to the judge, ma'am."

Gertrude Batista can't stay asleep. She's wired about getting out of Charlottesville and heading to the shore. Gertrude's just awakened from having a night sweat. At first she thought that she had peed in her sleep. The sheets are soaking wet and her pajamas are also. She needs to get out of bed, change the sheets, and change her night clothing. Thank God for short hair, it dries quickly.

Gertrude throws her comforter away from her and places her feet on the cold wooden floor. She immediately starts to shiver. *Good, at least the sweat has stopped. Damn these night sweats.* Gertrude changes and walks down the hall to check on Mrs. LaSlick. The lady isn't in her bed. Buddy, who has been sleeping in his bed, gets up and enters Mrs. LaSlick's room. Both leave the room and descend the stairs. *Jesus, where the hell can she be? God forbid, if she's left the house and is found two days from now frozen in a snow drift.*

"Mrs. LaSlick, where are you?" Gertrude starts turning on lights in the house. Entering the hall, Gertrude becomes aware of a small light on in the kitchen. Gertrude steps into the kitchen and finds her houseguest sitting at the kitchen table having a cup of tea.

"Oh, there you are...I was worried about where you might be."

"Well, honey, I decided to get up and come downstairs to make myself some tea. Would you like some?"

"OK. I'll pour myself some. I'm having problems sleeping."

"I hope that you aren't getting sick, honey."

"No....just some hormone problems."

"I recall those days."

"When you were going through menopause, did you take anything?"

"Honey, you're not going through menopause. You're having problems sleeping because you're pregnant with my grandchild."

"You know Mrs. LaSlick you're absolutely correct. I think that I'm going to go upstairs with my tea and drink it in bed. Why don't you do the same, we are leaving mighty early for the Eastern Shore tomorrow?"

The two strangers, a bond of gender, leave the kitchen with their cups of tea. *Thank God, I'm meeting Francie and Rick tomorrow. This is a living nightmare.*

Rick LaSlick thinks he's died and gone to heaven, although he feels that on some level he's committed a sin, doesn't know which commandment though, however; is in ecstasy that he pulled this one off. He drives to Beth's farm, leaps from his truck, runs up the front porch steps, slips and recovers as he gives the front door three quick loud raps.

Beth answers the door. "I see that you're happy."

"Damn right. I met two women, who were at the bar, treated them to drinks and dinner and gave the photo to the lady that lived in Oyster. Did you know that there's a lot of deputies out tonight as the women were stopped after leaving AJ's?"

"No. I wonder why?"

"It probably has to do with the stolen pictures. And I saw the lady and her friend, separated, sitting in the back seat of two squad cars. I smiled and waved."

"Rick that's terrible to do."

"I don't care. I got screwed and needed to get rid of it. My mother's coming tomorrow and I need to have my head on straight to figure out what's going on with her. I haven't called my dad yet, and I want to hear what mom has to say. I know one thing; she can't be traveling around the United States demented."

"Tomorrow's here, Rick, I was just turning in for the night. Want to stay over."

"That's a no brainer."

Rick and Beth hold hands as Beth busily turns lights off. They walk up the stairway leading to the master bedroom. It's a pretty crisp night so Beth's left the wood stove burning. The smell of wood adds a rustic fragrance to the house. Rick enjoys spending nights with Beth. He loves the coziness of her house and the luxury of her bed.

Jodi opens the door to the station and immediately sees Juney-Bea and Sally-Sue getting booked. *You have to be kidding....*she walks over to the shift commander.

"Hi Martin, what's going on? I know them."

"Ms. Karring is being processed for a DUI and possession of stolen property. And Ms. Moon has been arrested for possession of stolen property. Ms. Moon was holding a photograph taken by Frances Benjamin Johnston, when the deputy asked her to step from the car. It's the photo shown on the front page of our island newspaper and *The Washington Post.*"

"OK, thanks for the explanation...please continue..." Just as Jodi finish's her sentence her phone vibrates. "Hello."

"Jodi, this is Jane. I need to speak with you about Francie."

"What's the problem, Jane?"

"Francie never returned to the agency after going into the field. She hasn't picked up her dogs. Jon and I have them with us at our house. We are also concerned as to the whereabouts of Kaylee and Chip Wells."

"What?"

"I think that they're together somewhere in trouble. Francie would never leave her dogs."

"OK. Right now, there are a few active roadblocks. I will inform the night shift that they're missing. I wonder where they are. I'll give Greg Franks a call as he transported Francie in the field yesterday."

"Jon and I are worried sick. Come morning, we have to open our store, so we'll take Sergeant and Bella with us. Isn't Gertrude coming down?"

"I knew that she was supposed to be coming for Francie's birthday. So now that the snow's over, she most likely is. We need to find Francie prior to Gertrude's arrival. We don't need any more drama around here. Hopefully, Chip and Kaylee aren't missing."

Morning light and Juney Bea and Sally-Sue hear the change of shift and are anxious to post bond. What a miserable night they've spent sitting in a jail cell and not speaking. Juney Bea's so pissed that she's lost for words. Sally-Sue's trying to figure out how fucked she is.

The sun's rising and Gertrude and Mrs. LaSlick are travelling east on I-64 heading for the shore. Gertrude's deep in thought concerning the outcome of their meeting today. She plans to call Francie and inform her of this meeting since she was unable to reach her yesterday. Gertrude will call Rick again, just to touch base. They plan to meet at the agency at about noon. This meeting today needs to be productive as Gertrude has no plans of returning to Charlottesville with Mrs. LaSlick.

Kaylee and I have spent a miserable night sitting on the feed room floor with straw wrapped around us. We're shivering. The sound of unsettled horses is unnerving and the stench of manure, is overpowering. Kaylee and I have headaches. Odors sometimes set me off along with stress.

Kaylee has continued to cry. She sobbed throughout the night and I tried to comfort her. It didn't work. We both have cried for our mothers. I've said several decades of the rosary. Kaylee and I haven't heard the whimpering that we did hours earlier and fear the worst for Chip. In the distance we hear a dog yowling, and it upsets us. I figure that it's about dawn. I've wet my pants a couple of times. I'm certain that Kaylee has done the same.

The tack room door opens and the light is turned on. Two men are staring at us. One's holding duct tape. I make the sign of the cross. This is definitely not a good sign.

Jodi calls Greg Franks. "Greg, do you have any idea where Francie is?"

"What do you mean, isn't she at her home?"

"No. Weren't you out in the field with her yesterday?"

"Yes, and I left her in front of the agency. She said she had a hunch about the foals and needed to look something up on the computer. If she's missing I think that I may know where she is. Give me a few minutes and I'll meet you at the station."

"I'm already here Greg. It's been a long night."

"We'll find her." Greg hangs up and quickly grabs his pants, puts on his shirt, socks and shoes. He uses the bathroom, brushes his teeth and within fifteen minutes he's out of the house, sitting in his freezing vehicle.

A muscular man referred to as Vince, spins Kaylee around and duct tapes her wrists and mouth. When she turns and faces me, her eyes are saucers. Fear has turned her skin pure white. I'm nervous. I've begun to recite the rosary again. I'm sure to go to heaven for all the decades of the rosary said in the last few hours. I know that I should have gone to church last Sunday; I should have confessed to Father Grimes that the pot in the Biscotti jar was mine, but I never could figure out if having possession of pot is truly a sin, or not owning up to the matter is. I didn't steal the jar, Sally-Sue did and it wasn't my fault that there was a roadblock and she was arrested. The nuns used to drill, and I mean drill into our heads in Catholic elementary school, "Nobody can make you do anything." I would like the opportunity to argue the point. Let's take the position that I'm in currently. I will be forced to submit to duct tape. I can't run away from these thugs. This is definitely where I will be forced to do something that I don't want to do. These dudes look hard.

I'm shaking by the time Vince, spins me around, duct tapes my wrists and my mouth. I have had a phobia ever since I almost drowned in a pool as a kid. I don't like the feeling of not being able to breathe. I'm praying that I don't go into a full-blown panic attack. I don't have my stash of pot or tranquilizers.

Vince shoves Kaylee and I out of the tack room and slams the door behind us. I notice that Kaylee has peed in her pants as there's a circle around her butt. I must look the same. My pants are wet and cold as the snow outside of this barn.

Chip's in the aisle. He really looks in bad shape. He has a black eye and a bloody nose. His hands are taped behind him. There's another guy too. He smells like crap and has a black eye and a nose that looks as though it's been pounded into his face. If I didn't know better, I think that he's Mike Griffin, Brittany's fiancé. He's an islander and has a twin brother, Marty that I haven't seen in awhile. I think that Marty left the island and moved somewhere up north.

We're pushed from the barn and basically thrown into a red van. Kaylee and Chip are on the van's floor next to each other. Kaylee's crying and Chip really looks as though he needs medical attention. He's groaning and appears to be semi-conscious. Mike's thrown next to me on the floor. He isn't giving me any eye contact and I'm wondering what's up with him.

Greg picks up Jodi and travels to Temperanceville where Ms. Cary Sadie Nation-Savage lives. He remembered that Francie had noticed a barn in the distance and had questioned Ms. Cary Sadie Nation-Savage about it.

Greg turns down the snowy road and they begin their trek, passing a vacant log dwelling and coming to a barn. They notice fresh tire tracks in front.

"Greg, call this in. I have a feeling that there's going to be something awful behind those doors. I want several units here."

Greg calls dispatch, informing of his destination and requesting backup as Jodi gets out of the truck. He follows; both have pulled their Glock's. Greg steps to the side as Jodi opens the barn door. The smell of manure's overpowering. They enter, turn on lights and walk slowly, searching and moving their guns back and forth as they move forward. Jodi's stunned and notes that the horses have bags attached to them appearing to be collecting urine. The horses have no food or water. The smell is unbearable and the condition of the horses is horrendous.

Jodi makes her way to a closed door, and steps aside as she's announcing her presence. There's no noise. She opens the door and it's a feed closet. There's a pile of trampled straw in the corner. It appears as though somebody may have spent the night. She finds an additional light, turns it on and searches the floor. She kicks the straw and a cell phone moves into view. Jodi picks it up, opens it and notes that it's black and needs to be charged.

"Greg, I've found a cell phone. I think that it's Francie's. It's all beat up and looks like hers."

"I wonder who's in charge of this operation. I'm going to call Warren McKinney. These animals are in poor shape."

"Greg, we need to move quickly. I bet that Kaylee and Chip are with her."

As Greg and Jodi leave the feed closet, they see drops of blood on the barn floor.

"I hope that the blood I'm looking at isn't Francie's, Chip's or Kaylee's."

"My sentiment exactly, Greg."

Greg walks outside the barn and speed dials Warren McKinney.

"Warren, this is Greg Franks. You need to get out here to Temperanceville. We have found about twenty horses; in livestock stalls, with bags collecting their urine. There's no food or water for them and they are living in filth. If removal is warranted, we will need to obtain an order from the judge."

Greg's really upset. He's fallen in love with Francie, but hasn't said anything to her because he didn't want to scare her away. *I'm gonna hunt down the mother that did this and if she's injured the sonofabitch's gonna wish that he's secure in some jail far away from me.*

Warren takes a gulp of hot coffee. He's spent the night with Molly Smith and she's gotten up early to cook breakfast prior to leaving for work. Warren thought that this would be a calm morning.

"I have a pen and paper. Give me the address and I'll leave pronto." Molly overhears Warren as she sees him scribbling onto a small piece of paper.

Warren writes the address, gives Molly a kiss on the cheek, and as he's throwing on his coat, he says, "I think they've found the mares that delivered the foals. I'll call you later."

Warren doesn't warm his truck, uses an ice scraper doing a cursory job, backs out of Molly's driveway and is headed over the bridge within five minutes. *And I thought when I received this job; it would be a piece of cake. Where the hell am I going to place these mares? I'll need to contact some area horse rescue groups.*

20

Gertrude gives Rick LaSlick a phone call. She's just paid the toll at the Chesapeake Bay Bridge Tunnel and is nearing Cape Charles. Mrs. LaSlick has been humming *Amazing Grace* for two hours and Gertrude's about to backhand the bitch.

Rick's cell rings three times and then he picks up, "Hello."

"Yes, Rick LaSlick; Gertrude Batista. I've just reached the Eastern Shore so I should arrive at the agency in about two hours. We're going to stop for lunch. I've tried calling my daughter a couple of times, but she's hasn't answered her cell. We'll meet at the agency at about two."

"That's fine. And thank you for taking such good care of my mother."

"No problem." Gertrude clicks off her cell, has a hot flash, and sees a happy Mrs. LaSlick. Instantly, Gertrude feels guilty for her earlier thought of desiring to back hand this lady.

"Mrs. LaSlick, we're going to stop and have some lunch and then we'll be on our way again. I'm glad that you're enjoying yourself."

"I am dear. It's such a pretty area with snow and farm land. I haven't seen snow in many years and it reminds me of when I was a young girl, at home with my parents. Did I ever tell you about my mother's friend, Frances Benjamin Johnston? You know she's a famous lady, who took many pictures of places around here in the 1930's or so."

"No, I didn't know that ma'am."

Gertrude pulls into the parking area of The Chesapeake. It's her favorite restaurant with lots of local fresh fish. Gertrude helps Mrs. LaSlick out of the car and the two make their way slowly with Gertrude holding onto the elder along the snowy path leading to the restaurant. Mrs. LaSlick enters the restaurant smiling as there's a pleasant smell of fish and spices in the air. They sit at a booth, open their menus and stare marveling the menu.

"Look, they have some fish made Cajun style. How nice. No wonder Rick likes living around here."

They order Rock Fish, nicely spiced, with hush puppies, coleslaw and hot tea with lemon. Once finished, Gertrude pays the bill and both take a bathroom break.

Heading to the vehicle, Gertrude has a death grip on the old lady, intent on making sure that she doesn't fall and break a hip.

"Rick sure married well. You're such a nice person and I'm pleased that you are a part of my family."

Gertrude gives Mrs. LaSlick a smile as she buckles her seatbelt. Her neck's beginning to get hot, and she knows that a flash is coming. Gertrude has beads of sweat on her forehead and begins to grasp the steering wheel. *I wish that my daughter hadn't sent me that e-mail about Premarin. I'm in need of medication to ease these flashes, moods and sweats. I feel like killing somebody.*

It's about midday and Rick and Beth are enjoying each other's company They've just gotten out of bed for the second time and are back to eating. They've been using a lot of calories and need to replace the ones lost.

Rick looks outside. It's bright and sunny with winds coming from the south. Warmer breezes are mixing with colder ones, although it's only about a degree above freezing. Earlier in the morning, Beth made her goats a warm mash and fed them hay. In the house, there's a mixture of bacon, eggs, pancakes, coffee and love in the air.

"Do you feel less worried this morning, Rick?"

"Yes. I'm back on track again. I will never purchase anything from anybody that isn't standing behind a counter in a reputable store." Rick extends his hand and reaches for Beth patting her on the buttocks.

"What do you think is going to happen when you see your mother?"

"I don't know. My mother left my father thinking that he's been having an affair. I'm really concerned about mom's mental health. She would never have accused my father of cheating if she were in her right mind."

"I know. Dementia coupled with aging is difficult. Our short-term memory goes if we don't use it. For example do you know what you ate for breakfast yesterday?"

"Of course. Black coffee and with a nervous stomach I puked it." Rick pulls Beth to his lap, she sits, and he kisses her forehead.

"Well, that wasn't the best example."

Warren McKinney's as busy and overwhelmed as he has ever been. He arrives at the barn. Law enforcement and news media have gathered at this crime scene and it's a mess. He leaves his vehicle and proceeds to locate the sergeant in charge of this chaos.

"Sergeant, I'm with animal control."

"We've been waiting for you. It's horrible inside."

Warren's stomach suddenly is filled with acid.

"I was afraid of that. Has anybody taken photos, a video?"

"Yes, one of our deputy's has. His name is Minor and he's over there in front of the doors. He's the man not wearing his hat, waving it in front of his nose. Minor's breakfast is on the other side of the barn."

Warren excuses himself from the sergeant and walks over to Deputy Minor. As he approaches the barn he smells the noxious odor of a lot of manure.

"Deputy Minor, I'm Warren McKinney with animal control."

"It's good to meet you. I'm glad that you have the job to figure this out...not me."

"Sir, I'm wondering if you have taken any photos or videos of these horses."

"About an hour or so ago. We have taken and labeled videos as well as photos of each mare for documentation. And we left the mares as they were found so that you can see for yourself."

Warren breathes a sigh of relief. "Well, thanks...that will make my job a little easier."

The stressed warden walks into the barn and almost passes out. He takes one sniff of the stench and reaches for his Vicks VapoRub. It's what his mom rubbed under his nose and on his chest when he was a kid. With mares standing in their feces in livestock stalls attached to some device catching their urine, it's a gruesome sight. He walks down the aisle and counts twenty mares and in a large stall, four mares, not attached to any devices, standing in manure saturated with urine. These four mares are malnourished, their ribs are showing. There's no food seen for any of the horses, and no water.

Warren needs a game plan quickly. He turns to Deputy Minor. "Do you know who owns this barn?"

"Right now, Judge Longest. Prior to his leaving this morning for Christmas vacation he entered an order, giving us permission to search this place. Since it's a crime scene, we own it."

"Good. I need to find volunteers to detach the devices catching the mare's urine. We need to get a vet out here and Russ the blacksmith. I need a video going the whole time for when we find these assholes and have our day in court."

175

"What are your plans for the horses?"

"They are not in any shape for transportation. We're going to clean up this barn, have twenty-four-hour supervision, and get these mares healthy for adoption. This place has got to be one of those PMU barns and those four mares that aren't hooked up are probably the ones that had the foals. They may not make it by the looks of them."

Warren steps outside for a breath of fresh air and calls Doug Fields. Doug picks up on the second ring.

"Yeah...Doug here."

"Doug, Warren McKinney. We have a mess here in Temperanceville. I need a couple of stock trailers with hay brought here immediately. There are about twenty neglected mares. We've found the four mares that produced the foals. This is a Premarin farm."

"What...What the hell is that?"

"It's about using the urine of pregnant mares to make a pill for women who are going through their change. The urine helps to eliminate hot flashes."

"You can't be serious."

"As serious as a heart attack."

"I'll get right back with you Warren."

Doug Fields attempts to contact Mike Griffin who has a stock trailer. He leaves him a voice message. Doug decides to try Mike's girlfriend, Brittany. He calls Brittany.

"Hello, Brittany. This is Doug Fields. I'm looking for Mike and am unable to locate him."

"I don't know where he is and I don't care. I've broken off our engagement." He hears the click of her work landline.

Doug pauses for a moment. *Oh hell.* He gives Russ Trotter a call. He knows almost everybody in this area. Russ doesn't pick up and his cell goes to message mode.

"Hi Russ, this is Doug Fields. We have an emergency related to the foals. Give me a call as soon as possible."

Russ is at Elizabeth Allen's barn shoeing Francie's Batista's horse Trooper. Dr. Perry, a chiropractor has just left the barn after working on Trooper.

"Trooper isn't as stiff since Dr. Perry adjusted his spine. I'm going to clip a shoe on him. I think that if Francie has Dr. Perry come periodically he'll be balanced and we won't have an issue with Trooper, throwing his shoes." Russ feels his cell vibrating in his back jeans pocket.

"I have a call. Let me see who it is." Russ reaches in his pocket and sees the missed call. He recognizes the number as Doug Fields'.

"Doug Fields just gave me a call, Elizabeth. I wonder what's going on." Russ returns Doug's call.

"Hey Doug, what's up?"

"Hey, Russ. You won't believe this shit. Warren McKinney's at some barn in Temperanceville and has found about twenty mares neglected. We need you immediately at the barn. I'm on my way with a stock trailer of hay. We need another stock trailer filled with hay. Do you know anybody with enough to spare?"

"This is a bad time of year to be looking for hay. Everybody will be hoarding their supply especially after this blizzard."

"I know. Maybe if we ask a couple of farmers to give twenty bales of hay each, we can make due. This is a real mess. Russ, do you know Warren's phone number? You'll need to call him for the address."

"Yes. I'll give him a call now." He hangs up and speed dials Warren.

"Elizabeth you won't believe what's happened."

"Yes, Warren, this is Russ. I can come and help you. Have you called the vet?"

"Yes, I just spoke to Dr. Russell and he's on his way. This is a grisly situation Russ. You need to prepare yourself. It's a little tricky, let me give you the directions. Do you know where Carry Sadie Nation-Savage lives in Temperanceville?"

"Elizabeth, I'm leaving now. If you could find some hay and get your stock trailer heading for Temperanceville, I'd really appreciate it."

"OK. I'll give Beth a call and some of my neighboring farmers and I'll call you as I'm heading for Temperanceville."

Warren's organized. He has a game plan and his adrenaline is pumping. Molly's not going to believe him when he tells her what's happened. He's contacted the veterinarian and Dr. Russell has just arrived within a time span of fifteen minutes.

"Thanks for arriving so quickly Dr. Russell. This is a terrible situation, however; I'm becoming more organized by the minute. We are taking photos and a video continuously for documentation purposes."

"Alright, I hope that I have enough medication with me. You told me that there are about twenty neglected mares...and that this is a PMU farm."

"Yes. And I strongly believe that the four foals found in Assateague a couple of days ago are the foals of four severely neglected mares that are standing in a stall at the end of the barn without food or water."

As Dr. Russell enters the barn the stench overpowers him. He reaches for his Vicks...a true veteran. Warren and he enter the first livestock stall and Warren helps to detach the Urine Collection Device. The mare's in poor shape. She has multiple lesions of a bacterial infection surrounding her urethra where the device was implemented.

Everybody's working quickly and diligently. Stalls along the walls of the barn are cleaned and fresh straw found in the feed closet is spread around stalls. Feed buckets and water buckets are cleaned and water's placed in stalls. Some of the livestock stalls are dismantled so that larger stalls are constructed. Dr. Russell continues treating each mare. Some mares are too weak to walk to their clean stalls. He begins hydrating by the use of IV's.

Warren's phone rings and it's Doug Fields. "I'm on my way with a stock trailer of good orchard grass. Give me the location in Temperanceville."

Warren completes his call and returns to help the vet. He and Dr. Russell are viewing the four mares that weren't hooked up to the Urine Collection Device. Two of the mares are down. Dr. Russell enters the stall. The one mare's dead...no flesh...bones. The other he puts humanely down. It's questionable if the remaining will pull through.

21

Mike's miserable. He's in a van, an unwilling passenger, duct taped with others; Francie, Kaylee and some other dude that he doesn't know. Mike's filthy. He's been bound for two days, hasn't had anything to eat or drink, is dehydrated and stinks.

He knows the guy driving. Vince Belli, a tall, tough and dishonest dude. His passenger is Sal Rigatoni the brains of this operation. He's a dabbler; a gambler who enjoys a quick buck. Why he ever listened to his brother, Marty. *Quick money. Keep an eye on the mares and make five hundred dollars a week. Bullshit.*

Mike glances at Kaylee and Francie. They're scared to death. Kaylee looks as if she's going to pass out and Francie's breathing heavily. Francie looks as though she's about to have a panic attack. The young guy with them has a black eye and looks as if he's suffering from a migraine from hell. He's slumped over leaning on Kaylee, moaning.

The van takes a quick left and everybody falls over. I'm afraid that we're going to be murdered. I'm phobic. With tape over my mouth and my hands bound I'm very close to meltdown stage. I've wet my pants for the third time hours ago. My pants are cold and wet. I need to remain calm and figure out where the hell we're going. I really don't know this area of the shore; it's not my turf for investigations.

I notice that the water's on my right and I've seen a small sign, Quinby. I've never heard of the place. It looks pretty isolated. I've taken a look at Chip. He doesn't look good. His eye's oozing, swollen and has bled. Chip's been groaning again and is leaning on Kaylee who looks like she's about to faint. She has no color in her face and her eyes are very wide.

I'm wondering what Mike's doing with us. I think that it is him, even though he looks pretty rough. I've seen him around with his fiancée Brittany. An item...a handsome couple. They were engaged a few months ago. Brittany's been strutting around the island showing her ring...a very large diamond. She's the envy of other young island girls. I have a feeling that Mike is involved with this PMU operation. He's probably making some side money as the diamond purchased for his love, is real expensive. I've come to the conclusion that Mike deserves what he gets from these thugs. I don't and neither does Kaylee and Chip.

I look over at Chip again. He really is in need of medical assistance, his eye and nose has started to bleed again. He's stopped moaning and his breathing is labored.

The vehicle stops. The driver, Vince gets out. I'm really anxious and my breathing has become more labored. Kaylee's eyes are those of bewilderment. Chip's still out of it.

The other guy gets out. I think his name is Sal as I've heard the two talking. They are not from here and have a distinct accent, somewhere from the north. Sal's dressed for a fashion show. With a tan cashmere coat, black leather gloves and shoes, he's stylish and to boot has stolen my brown shawl that mom made. He has folded it and is wearing it as a scarf. That's a real kick...stealing from the victim. What balls!

Vince opens the back door and yanks Mike out like he's a sack of flour. Mike hits the frozen ground with a thud. Vince gives Mike a kick in the ribs for good measure. Mike doubles up in a fetal position and groans.

Vince grabs Kaylee who's holding onto Chip. They're flung from the van, tossed like garbage and land onto the icy ground. Chip hits his head as Kaylee tries in vain to hold onto him. Kaylee begins to sob and plead for their life. Vince grins.

I'm thrown from the van. I land flat on my back and slide on some ice. I've hit the back of my head on ice and am feeling dizzy as I hear the van doors close and see the back of the vehicle as it leaves us stunned. All I know is that we've been left somewhere near Quinby. I can see some water to my right.

Marty Griffin arrives at the sheriff's station. He's ready to come clean. As he walks in the front doors, he notices Brittany on the far right. She's looking hot. Tight leather skirt, with a violet sweater and cowboy boots. Marty walks over to Brittany. He surprises her.

"Marty, what the hell are you doing here. I thought you were in Miami employed as a lifeguard."

"Brittany, I need to speak with a deputy. Something has happened. Why are you wearing sunglasses?"

"Well, your asshole for a brother beat me up. I'm done with him."

"By the way, I've been unable to reach Mike for the last two days. Do you know where he is?"

"Nope."

Marty gets a knot in his stomach. He has a feeling that *shits going down and he's betting his brother's caught in it.*

"I need to file a police report."

"What the hell's going on Marty?"

"You'll be hearing about it soon enough. Who's in charge?"

"Captain Jodi Burgess, however; she's not here. Does this have anything to do with horses?"

"Yes, it does."

"I'll go and get the person next in line to take the police report." Brittany walks swiftly from the waiting area and returns with a deputy.

"Deputy Sean Pleasants this is Marty Griffin. He is the twin brother of Mike, the person I was engaged to. He says that he needs to make a police report."

"OK. Follow me to one of our conference rooms."

Deputy Pleasants and Marty walk to one of the conference rooms near the waiting area. Marty follows and closes the door. Deputy Pleasants has a notepad and pen out ready for the report. Marty knows that he will be arrested, however; he needs to find his brother.

"Mr. Griffin what may I do for you sir."

"Please call me Marty."

"Marty, please inform me as to why you're here and why you want to file a report."

"Well, sir, this is a very long story."

"I have all day." Deputy Pleasants lowers himself in his chair, clears his throat and taps his pen on the wooden table.

"Alright. Please keep up with me as this story is twisted."

"Go for it."

"OK. One year ago, I was a lifeguard up in Atlantic City. Do you ever go to Atlantic City to watch shows and gamble?"

"Let's talk about you and keep to the story."

"Well, although I was a lifeguard, I enjoy betting on horses, buying lottery tickets and gambling at the casinos. It's a fast paced life."

"What does this have to do with anything Mr. Griffin?"

"One day at the track, I met this dude named Sal Rigatoni."

"Is that his real name?"

"Yeah. He's Italian from New Jersey."

"Keep going...."

"We had just bet on a two year old, Good as Gold that won. Sal's made some big money on horses and we're waiting in line to get our pay-off and he asks me if I'd like to join him for a few

183

drinks. What the hell. I'm feeling happy; I've just won about five-hundred on a long shot. Anyway, we go to Jerry's a corner bar and I get plastered. Sal starts talking about pregnant mares and using their urine for women's hot flashes, you know urine in a pill. The pill's called Premarin. He said that he was in the business and needed somebody to oversee his operation on the Eastern Shore. Sal said that his parents had a place on the Eastern Shore and he was going to use their barn. His parents don't visit often. He wondered if I'd be interested. Fast money, you bet. I told him that I have a twin brother that lives in Chincoteague. Oh, by the way, my brother and Brittany were engaged, but I just found out that they've broken up. I wonder if she'll give the diamond back."

"Mr. Griffin, Marty...let's stay on track here." Deputy Pleasants says as he takes a sip of Coke.

"Alright, I introduced Mike to Sal and his right hand man, Vince Belli and my brother's supposed to check on the mares. He's to be paid five-hundred a week."

Deputy Pleasants is quickly taking notes. He yawns and takes a sip of his soda.

"What I'm trying to tell you sir, is that I got in way over my head. Those four foals, Sal and Vince got rid of them...unloaded them in Assateague. I wrote the note to the park ranger. I didn't want them to die. I just happened to be down here when the mares gave birth. It was atrocious. Babies ripped away from their mothers. When I witnessed that I threw up. I didn't realize. I never thought about foals, just pregnant horse urine. I've been trying to reach my brother for a couple of days now and there's no answer at his home or his cell. He's missing. I want to complete a report or whatever to get you to find him. He's my twin, my only sibling."

Deputy Pleasants shifts his weight from one elbow to the other as he continues to take notes. "Mr. Griffin, we are aware of this situation, although didn't have names. We are looking for a social worker named Francie Batista. Do you have any idea where she is?"

"No, I don't know a social worker. Why do you think that she is involved?"

"Let me ask the questions. Your brother's missing and you want out of this business, is that correct?"

"Well, yes…but I was not in this business my brother is."

"From the information that I've received the mares have been neglected. You obviously were around when the foals were born and snatched and left to die. I am going to hold you until I discuss charges with our Commonwealth Attorney. For now, you will remain here. I will be getting back with you within the hour."

Deputy Pleasants pushes his chair back, stands, and gathers his notes and leaves. Mike sits with his hands cupped over his forehead. He has a pulsating migraine.

22

Gertrude Batista arrives in Chincoteague. She parks behind the agency near the library and helps Mrs. LaSlick out of the vehicle. There's a man, sitting on a bench by the library. He's well dressed for the weather, nice leather jacket, boots, leather gloves and hat. He has his face towards the sun appearing to be enjoying its warmth. Mrs. LaSlick sees her son.

"Bonjour my baby."

"Madre, how are you?"

"Fine."

Gertrude walks to Rick and extends her hand. "I presume that you are Rick LaSlick."

"Yes. And you must be, Gertrude Batista. I would like to thank you for taking care of my mother and pay you for your service."

"No, thanks. I want us to discuss this situation with my daughter, Francie. I'm anxious to see her as I missed her birthday two days ago. I've been trying to reach her throughout the day to no avail, to make sure that she's available."

The three continue to walk. Rick's holding onto his mother's left elbow. He's fearful that she's going to fall on black ice. Gertrude's holding her too. The alligator bag's hitting Gertrude in her hip as they walk. The trio reaches the agency and the door is locked. Gertrude's stomach flutters.

"How about if we walk to the corner? There's a bookstore and Francie's close friends are there. They might know where my daughter is."

They continue walking and reach Sundial Books. Gertrude enters and sees Jane sitting behind the counter.

"Hi Jane!

Jane smiles as she looks to her side. Gertrude sees Jon walking from the back of the store with Francie's dogs, Sergeant and Bella.

"Hi Jon! I'm looking for my daughter. We're supposed to be meeting with her today over at the agency."

Gertrude walks up to the dogs whose tails are wagging and Bella begins yowling. She gets on her knees, pets and kisses the dogs. "Oh, I'd like to introduce you to Mrs. LaSlick and her son, Rick."

Rick shakes hands with Jane and Jon. Mrs. LaSlick walks over to the children's corner and shuffles through some children's books. She sees a small chair, picks up the newspaper, and settles in. Rick stands next to the front door near his mother and looks out the window at the Roxy Theater.

"I see that you have Francie's dogs so I'm assuming that my daughter's stuck in the field with a home visit?"

Jane walks towards Gertrude. "How about if we go to the sun porch for a moment?"

Gertrude pulls away. "Why? What's the matter? Oh my God, something has happened to my daughter!"

Rick looks at Jon, whose walking towards Gertrude. "Where's my daughter?" Gertrude says as she sways and the room goes black.

We are cold, duct taped and I'm freezing. Chip's not well. He's semi-conscious and Kaylee's about to have a meltdown as she tries to keep him as warm as possible. I walk towards Kaylee. I have to at least get this blasted tape off my mouth. I don't think that we can get the tape from our bound hands, which are behind us and multi-layered, but it's worth a try. I can't stand this bound feeling.

I look at Kaylee and talk with my eyes. I bend over behind her hands and nudge her bound hands trying to get her to tug the tape from my mouth. Kaylee gets what I'm trying to direct her to do. *Thank you God...thanks Saint Anthony...*She struggles, twisting and wiggling her fingers over my mouth. She finds the end of the tape, holds and I pull away. I scream in pain as the tape rips from my mouth. "Thank you Kaylee! My God that was tough."

Kaylee bends her face to my taped hands. I move my fingers around trying to find the end of her tape. I'm finally able to find the end and I give it a pull. Kaylee flinches as the tape tears her skin and lips while I struggle to pull. Finally, the tape's off. She screams as I rip over her lips. Mike flinches and looks away.

Mike's next. I help him to get rid of the tape binding his face. He's pretty messed up, although not as bad at Chip. It looks like somebody's used him as a punching bag. He doesn't utter a word as the tape is removed.

We decide to leave Chip as is. He doesn't have tape covering his mouth. He's been pretty badly beaten. We're not going to stress him by doing anything to him. Blood continues to flow from his eyes, nose and recently his mouth.

"I think that one of you needs to stay behind with this guy while one of you walks with me to find help." Mike says.

"Mike, I think that you're referring to this *guy* who happens to be my co-worker Chip Wells. Let me introduce you to my friend, Kaylee. She's with the local humane society. By the way, what the hell are you doing here? I'll bet a year's salary that you have something to do with this situation that we're in, neglect to horses and those four abandoned foals."

"Your good at fitting pieces together Francie. I recall how well you did with the Eastern Shore Wind Chime Killer a year ago." Mike sneers.

"Fuck you, Mike. Bart almost killed me while I was vacationing in Key West. Anyway, I don't think that you're in any position to cop an attitude. In fact, I think that you're in deep shit or should I say manure!"

"Whatever. I'll tell you I was involved. I've been making good money. This is a very profitable business, Premarin; with all these women going through menopause and needing relief."

"Oh, so you're a menopausal woman's knight in shining armor. How thoughtful of you to want to help. And I would guess that you're the insensitive asshole that left the four foals dying at the Coral Pen in a blizzard."

"No. I wasn't a part of that."

"Well, it still doesn't make you less guilty."

Russ's cell phone rings, and Doug Fields is on the other end talking to somebody. Russ interrupts. "Yeah, what's up?"

"Have you spoken with Warren?"

"Yeah...a second ago. I'm on my way. Elizabeth's cleaning her stock trailer and is going to call some neighbors and fill the trailer with hay. Did you hear from Mike yet?"

"No. He's nowhere to be found. I spoke to Brittany and she hung up on me...says that they have broken up."

"Hey, Doug, I think that I'm almost to the barn as there's tons of police and media."

"You're getting there before me. Did you know that somebody was arrested last night with one of those stolen photos by Frances Johnston?"

"No. I had read about the lady...and photos. Who was arrested?"

"Do you remember the social worker supervisor, Sally-Sue Moon and her supervisor, Juney Bea Karring?"

"Yeah. Wasn't Moon Francie Batista's supervisor?"

"You got it right…and she pulled time for possession of pot."

Russ turns into the dirt road leading to the barn. "Well, they were stopped for running a red light on Chincoteague and Karring was popped with a DUI and Moon was found holding the photo."

"No shit. I remember Moon went to jail because of the hidden pot in the Biscotti jar. She always claimed innocence."

"Listen Russ, I need to pay attention as this trailer's swaying. I'll see you in about twenty minutes."

Russ arrives at the barn and is escorted inside by Deputy Minor. Once entering Russ is shocked by the chaos, smell and atrocious living conditions. He locates Warren and Dr. Russell who is removing a device catching urine.

"Hello, Warren. I've just arrived. What's the first item that you want me to do?"

"Hi. Russ. Thanks for arriving so quickly. Do you know Dr. Russell?"

"Yes. Our paths have crossed numerous times."

"Dr. Russell, what horse do you want Russ to trim first?"

"Russ. All of the horses' hooves need trimming. God knows when they had a trim. Photos and a video needs to be used when you are trimming. Let me know what horses need more than a trim."

"We need to take really good notes and have continuous documentation for the trial, when we find the bastards who did this." Warren says as he proceeds to lift the back leg of a bay mare."

OK. I'll get started at the far end of the barn. Does anybody have any Vicks?"

Six bottles are thrown to Russ, who skillfully ducks, picks the closest bottle, opens it and smears a glob under his nose. "Thanks…now I can get to work!"

Doug Fields arrives with hay and Elizabeth follows him down the dirt road passing the log cabin. They quickly become aware of the magnitude of what's happening. Doug and Elizabeth park their trailers and meet with Deputy Minor at the front door of the barn.

"Warren's in there…he's with Dr. Russell and Russ. They will inform you as to where the hay needs to be delivered. We're here to help with that."

Elizabeth enters with Doug following. She sees the crime scene, smells death and falls to her knees crying. Doug's shocked by the brutality of it and leans to comfort Elizabeth. Deputy Minor witnesses Elizabeth's despair and comes to her aid.

"Doug, why don't we escort Elizabeth outside and she can sit in her truck and we'll unload her hay first. This is too much for her to handle."

"Damn right. It's almost too much for me to handle. Do you happen to have a cigarette?"

"No. I quit smoking about three months ago. I know how you are feeling as I could light up right this second…although I don't think folks smoke around a barn."

Deputy Minor and Doug help Elizabeth to her truck.

"Elizabeth I know that this is a shock. Just sit here. You don't need to do anything and we will put the hay up once we're told the spot."

"I'm sorry. I just didn't realize the degree of neglect. I can't handle seeing these beautiful horses so mistreated. It's just not fair."

Russ is busy working on the horses when he is summoned by one of the deputy's. Elizabeth is outside and Russ needs to speak with her. As Elizabeth sees Russ, she begins to cry. Russ rushes to Elizabeth to comfort her. Russ opens the truck's passenger side door, and slides in. He holds Elizabeth and gently kisses her forehead. Doug and Deputy Minor leave.

"I know that this is very upsetting Elizabeth. How about if I detach the trailer and you drive home? I'll come by after I'm finished trimming the horses."

"I'm in a state of shock. I can't get over the vision in my mind and the smell. I just didn't know that it was this bad." Elizabeth buries her head in Russ's chest and sobs.

"I think that I'll call Beth and ask her to come and pick you up. We can return for your trailer and truck later. I think that Beth will make you feel better."

"I think so. I just don't feel as though I'm able to drive."

Russ dials Beth's number as he continues to hold Elizabeth. "Beth, Russ. Elizabeth's at a barn in Temperanceville where a bunch of horses have been found neglected. If you could drive over and pick her up, I'd appreciate it. She's very upset and can't drive."

"No problem. Does this have to do with the four foals?"

"Yep. And when you arrive you're not going into the barn. Let me give you the address. I'll see you in about fifteen minutes."

Russ continues to hold Elizabeth. She's pretty pale and is shaking. Deputies have started to remove the hay from her stock trailer. A reporter comes to the truck.

"How about an interview? I haven't been permitted inside of the barn."

Russ shakes his head and holds onto Elizabeth as he doesn't want her face plastered on the six o'clock news.

Beth arrives and Russ continues to shield Elizabeth's face as he carefully walks her to Beth's truck. Beth looks stunned.

JIGSAW Teresa Adele Bettino

There are sheriff deputies and medical personnel all over the place. She makes a quick turn and leaves.

Russ walks back to the barn, takes a whiff and grabs his bottle of Vicks.

23

Jodi and Greg have left the crime scene and are returning to Chincoteague to meet with Marty Griffin, whose about to be charged with animal abuse and neglect. Jodi's cell rings; she looks at the number and realizes that it's Jane. "Hi Jane. Has Francie shown up?"

Jane diverts her eyes from Gertrude, whose sitting in a chair holding a glass of water, "No, but her mother's here and is recovering from the shock of her daughter's disappearance. She fainted. Would you like to speak with Gertrude?"

"Yes, I may be able to calm her down a bit." Jodi says as Jane quickly walks over to Gertrude and hands her the phone.

"Hello." Gertrude says with a quivering voice. She takes a delicate sip of water.

"Hi Gertrude, this is Jodi."

"What's happened to my daughter? Is some lunatic running around here again on a killing spree?"

"No, Gertrude. I feel certain that Francie had a hunch about where the four abandoned foals came from. Have you ever heard of Premarin?"

"You can't be serious. I've been taking it for hot flashes."

"Well, Francie figured that the foals were PMU babies and she most likely told Kaylee and Chip. They drove to a barn in Temperanceville to take a look."

"Did you go to the barn to search for them?"

"Yes.

"Was Francie there?"

"No."

In the background Jodi hears Gertrude scream. The cell makes a thumping noise as Jodi holds the phone away from her ear. "Gertrude, we're on our way. I'll see you in about ten minutes."

Jon and Jane are attempting to get Gertrude to relax. Jane bends to pick up the cell phone from the floor as Mrs. LaSlick screams, "Mon Dieu, Oh my God, Rick. It's her on the front page...Frances Benjamin Johnston...her photos stolen. She was my mother's friend."

Gertrude, Jane, Jon and Rick look at Mrs. LaSlick.

"Your mother knew Frances Johnston?" Jon asks surprised with eyebrows raised.

"Yes. My grandmother and Ms. Johnston became friends when Frances Johnston moved to New Orleans. My mother inherited the photos after my grandmother died in about 1965."

"Well, she's an icon here. Ms. Johnston came to the Eastern Shore in about 1930 and stayed in a hotel in Accomack County. She basically traveled the shore taking photos of buildings, farms and mills. She donated her photos to the Library of Congress. A couple of weeks ago they were stolen." Jon says, as he's walking over towards a bookshelf. He chooses an art book and begins shuffling through pages.

Rick looks away from his mother. He's looking out the window across the street at the theater. The movie tonight is *La Cage aux Folles*... the cage with the insane ones. Rick starts perspiring and takes off his coat, hat, and gloves, placing them on floor by his mother.

A deputy enters the store and Sergeant and Bella wag tails and greet the customer. The air within Sundial Books is thick...stress...negative energy. Sergeant jumps onto the deputy wanting a good ear rub.

"You must have a dog?" Gertrude says holding a tissue, eyes red from crying.

"Yes, I do. I have two dogs and a couple of island cats."

"Good for you." Gertrude claps getting Sergeant's attention. He readily comes to her along with Bella.

"Can I help you with anything, Kirk?"

"No. I'm just looking for a book to purchase for my wife for Christmas. Jane do you have any suggestions?"

"What type of book does she like to read?"

"Oh. I think fiction, maybe a little bit of mystery."

"We could probably write a mystery right now." Jon looks across the room to the children's section of the store, "Mrs. LaSlick is from New Orleans and her mother was friends with Frances Benjamin Johnston. She's just informed us that her mother was a friend of Ms. Johnston's when Ms. Johnston lived in New Orleans." Jon walks toward Rick and his mother. Rick continues to look out the window.

"We've just arrested the persons that were in possession of one of the stolen photos, two women, Sally-Sue Moon and Juney Bea Karring."

Silence...Gertrude recovers two heartbeats later. Rick's looking pale eyeing the room, staring at his mother as additional perspiration beads form on his forehead.

"What the hell are they doing on the island? I thought Sally-Sue was in jail for pot possession." Gertrude shrills as Rick can be heard clearing his throat.

"She pulled her time, came back yesterday. Sally-Sue had a meeting with Captain Burgess."

"What do you think that the meeting was about?"

"I heard through the grapevine...she wants an investigation about who put the pot in the Biscotti jar."

Jon lets out a yip...Jane looks over to him shaking her head in disapproval.

"So, let me get this straight...deputy, um...Kirk, she wants Jodi to investigate whose pot was in the jar, when she was the one that took the jar from Wanda Burton's desk. I wonder just who she thinks it is. And now, she's back with her friend, Juney Bea and they've been arrested for having stolen property…namely Frances Benjamin Johnston's photos. This is totally unreal." Gertrude says and then screams, "You know what I need? I need a good stiff drink instead of this nasty water."

Jane walks toward Gertrude. She notices that Rick's back is again turned away from those in the room. She attempts to engage him in conversation. "Rick, what do you think about all this commotion on Chincoteague Island?"

Rick shifts, looks at his mother sitting on a chair in the children's section of Sundial Books. His sweet mother's clutching the newspaper to her breast. He smiles. Takes another look at the Roxy and says, *"La Cage aux Folles"* and his mother hysterically laughs. He sighs and continues, as all stare. "I've recently relocated to the Eastern Shore and have been enjoying living here, although lately the weather's been a shock for someone who's lived their entire life in New Orleans." He walks to his mother and kneels, holding her hands. "I do know about the stolen photos as I read the newspapers and was aware of Frances Johnston through my mother inheriting some photos."

Gertrude walks to the door opens it, looks up and down Main Street, takes three deep breaths and closes the door. Hot flashes are taking a hold of her. Kirk, the deputy, smiles and continues to look at Rick.

"However; I guess that I don't know the history of Chincoteague as I don't know Sally-Sue Moon and Juney Bea Karring and therefore don't have a frame of reference as to this humor surrounding a stolen Biscotti jar. I'm here in an attempt to figure out my mother's situation with social worker, Francie Batista, who presently appears to have be missing."

"Well, said my son." Rick smiles at his mother and gives her a kiss on her cheek.

The door opens and Captain Jodi Burgess and Deputy Greg Franks enter. Kirk nods realizing that he needs to disappear, and leaves the room, heading for the fiction section of the store. Jodi walks towards Gertrude and embraces her.

"Jodi, where's my daughter."

"I don't know."

"I hear that Sally-Sue and Juney Bea are back?"

"Well, yes. Sally-Sue's returned to the shore from Goochland yesterday. She and I have spoken. She wanted the sheriff's department to investigate whose stash of pot it was in the Biscotti jar. I told her no."

"And now I hear that she's been arrested along with her sidekick Juney Bea for possession of stolen property."

"Yes. I've just had an update. She says that she met a guy named Sal Rigatoni, from New Jersey and that he gave it to her as a present. As you may know, we've been doing roadblocks trying to find your daughter, Kaylee and Chip Wells as well as any of the stolen property from the Library of Congress. Juney Bea ran a red light, was charged with drunk driving and possession of stolen property and Sally-Sue has been charged with possession of stolen property. They are sitting in jail. A preliminary hearing is scheduled for tomorrow."

Kirk returns. "I really need to be getting back to work. I've found two books by Virginia authors; one is about the Eastern Shore Wind Chime Killer and the other by Loretta Walls, *Rendezvous*. I really think that my wife's going to enjoy these books. Imagine that... somebody's already written about what happened last year on the Eastern Shore and is capitalizing on it. The book *Rendezvous* looks interesting... something about a perfume company. God knows my wife loves to read."

Kirk moves towards the register as Jane walks behind the counter. Kirk's paying for his books when two men walk into the store. Sergeant and Bella growl as Rick stands up stares at the men and clears his throat. He resumes his vigilant stance facing the window looking onto Main Street.

"Hello. How may I help you?" Jon exclaims as he walks towards the door.

"We're looking for a computer. Do you happen to have one?"

"No, but the library does. A few buildings to your left as you leave by the front door."

"Excuse me, sir. Where did you get the folded shawl that you have around your neck? That's my daughter's!"

"What!" Jane and Jon exclaim.

Captain Jodi Burgess pulls her gun...Deputy Greg Franks pulls his. Kirk drops his books, pulls his Glock as Mrs. LaSlick stands up. She attempts to walk to her son, takes two steps and falls.

The men turn to leave. Rick, side steps, sticks out his leg and trips one of the men. He falls to the floor as Jodi moves forward. Sergeant leaps onto the man on the floor, lifts his leg peeing on the guys black leather coat. Rick grabs the guy's arms as Jodi moves to further subdue and cuff him.

"Sergeant come!" Gertrude shrieks as she watches the other guy open his coat.

Jane sees the gun, dives under the counter as Bella leaps over Jodi. Bella bites the gunman's arm and continues to hold. The gun falls to the floor as Greg wrestles him to the floor. Rick grabs the gun and attempts to pull Bella off the guy. It doesn't work. Bella's not letting go.

"Alright. I give up. Get this fucking dog off of me."

"Bella come!" Jon says as Kirk and Greg cuff the dude.

Bella releases her grip and returns to Sergeant whose sitting next to Gertrude. With the last guy cuffed, Rick helps his mother from the floor. He moves her chair closer to the window. "Sit…and don't get up."

"My, my; and who do we have here, I wonder." Jodi says breathlessly. With the men standing and cuffed, Kirk and Greg, look in their pockets for some identification. "Jon please lock your front and back doors as we don't need any more surprises."

Kirk finds a wallet in the pocket of the black leather worn by the pissed on stranger. Greg locates a wallet in the cashmere coat of the gun toting stranger wearing Francie's shawl. Kirk reads the license, "Vince Belli from Atlantic City, New Jersey and Greg chimes in, "Sal Rigatoni. And take a guess where he's from…of course, Atlantic City."

I'm schlepping with Mike trying to find a house, store or whatever to help us. Kaylee's back where we were dropped, taking care of Chip, who really needs medical attention. He awoke prior to us leaving and has a bewildered look on his face.

"Mike, do you know what direction we're walking."

"Why? What the fuck does it matter?"

"You know. You better clean up your act."

"Screw yourself."

We continue to walk in silence. He trips and falls with his hands bound behind. Standing again will be difficult for the prick with all the snow and ice. I continue to walk without helping him. He's the biggest asshole on the Eastern Shore and to be stuck with him, how horrible.

I hear traffic, so I walk toward sound and come across a small road with a farmhouse. I walk up to the farmhouse and kick at the door. There's a car outside, so I'm hopeful somebody's home. Mike has caught up with me. He's wet...of course still smelly and has snow in his hair. He must have rolled.

The door opens and a kid about nine appears. "Hello, is your momma home?"

Big eyes look at us as the kid spins leaving us at the door. I look at Mike and snarl. "Keep your foul mouth shut or I'll kick you in the nuts." I face the door as I hear footsteps. I don't want this woman freaking out, slamming the door and running away with her kid. A young woman comes to the door. Her hair is long and stringy and her clothing wrinkled.

"Hello, ma'am. We need your help. Can you please call the police and also ask them to bring an ambulance."

The woman looks like she's had a visit from a dead relative. "Ma'am did you hear me?"

The kid steps next to his mom. "Mom's deaf."

Mike laughs; I turn and kick him in the nuts. He's now groaning.

"May I come in and use your phone? You do have a telephone, maybe a landline or cell?"

The kid lets me in the house and I follow his mother down the hallway. This kid's smart, he shuts the door, locking Mike outside, doubled over on the front porch.

I reach the kitchen; the woman removes the tape from my wrists. I dial 9-1-1. Dispatch picks up.

"Hi. This is Francie Batista. I've been kidnapped and am with others. We need an ambulance as soon as possible. Please come to this address where I'm calling from. Let me put a family member on the phone so that he can tell you where I am."

I hand the phone over. His mom's looking out of the foyer window staring at Mike. She is smiling. The kid hangs up the phone and comes to me. "Where's your father?"

"He left about a month ago. He has a girlfriend."

"Oh. I'm sorry. What's your name?

"Larry Smith."

"And your mom, what's her name?"

"Alice."

"Does your mom work?"

"Nope."

"I'm a social worker. Maybe I can help your mother?"

"You're the one that needs help...not us." *My... he's perceptive.*

"How about if I return next week, after I look better and we can talk about what's going on?"

"I don't think so. We're moving in a few days."

"Oh. Is it around here?"

"Nope."

Jodi's standing in Sundial Books. The two suspects are cuffed and everybody's waiting for back-up to arrive. Rigatoni's smart. He's not saying anything. His friend, Vince is looking nervous.

"Hey you...over there looking out the window. Didn't I meet you at AJ's, sitting at the bar and we had a few?"

"I don't think so."

"Yeah...aren't you Cajun or something like that?"

"I haven't met you...end of conversation."

Jodi's speaking with Brittany. "Please read the arrest report on Sally-Sue Moon. I seem to recall the name Sal Rigatoni."

"Jodi, the report says that she met this guy from New Jersey named Sal Rigatoni, who gave her the photo of the grist mill as a gift for her Oyster house."

"That's what I thought. Thanks Brittany."

"Mr. Rigatoni, I understand that you like photographs. Does the name Sally-Sue ring a bell? Sally-Sue says that she met you last night and that you gave her a photo as a gift."

"I don't know what you're talking about. I want my lawyer. I do get one call."

"Yeah...your rights have been read."

"Where's my daughter? You have the shawl that I made for her last year. What did you do with my daughter? Listen you sonofabitch, you low life Italian, I'm gonna make some calls. I'll call my uncle...he'll take care of you and Vinnie. If my daughter has one hair out of place...you better be looking over your shoulder, you traditore! You know, in Virginia unlike New Jersey we utilize the death penalty here."

"Like I said, I want my lawyer."

"You can take your attorney and shove him up your ass. I want my daughter now!"

Rick walks over to his mother. He helps her up and speaks to Jodi. "My mother is very old and she is tired. She's already fallen and this is very stressful as well as confusing for her. I don't feel that it is beneficial in any way for my mother to be a part of this. I am therefore requesting Captain Burgess that we be excused. I would like to take my mother to my house, and once Francie Batista is located, I would be more than agreeable to meet with whomever concerning the well-being of my mother."

Jodi nods. "Yes, you and your mother may leave.

Rick makes no eye contact with either of the men. He puts his coat on, holds his hat and gloves and helps his mother with her coat and escorts her.

Jon unlocks the door.

"Hey dude...I do know you. I can't recall your name."

"No sir. I don't know anybody from Atlantic City."

Gertrude gets up from her chair and speaks with Rick. "I have a few possessions of your moms. They're in the car in the back seat. I didn't lock the car, so feel free to take them."

"Thanks for helping my mother."

"You're welcome." Gertrude gives Mrs. LaSlick a hug.

He and his mother leave. Rick carefully walks holding onto his mother's elbow as they amble behind the library. They reach Gertrude's car and Rick grabs the rest of his mother's possessions. He helps his mother into the front seat and places a seat belt across her. Rick kisses his mother on her forehead and races around the vehicle, hops in and cranks the engine. He quickly peels from the parking lot, makes a left onto Main, passes the theater and laughs...*yes...birds of a feather...they stick together*...and as he's headed over the bridge, Rick gives Beth a call. She doesn't pick up and he leaves a message.

"Beth, I'm heading to Norfolk. I have my mom and I'm taking her home. Take care of my house and don't tell anybody where I am. I'll explain later."

24

Sirens can be heard in the distance and within a few minutes pull up to the weathered looking farmhouse. Mike's still on the porch, clutching his privates as the deputy gets out of his vehicle. The ambulance arrives and I walk from the house.

I speak to the deputy. The deputy cuts Mike's tape. I look to Mike and point. "This guy, with me has something to do with the neglect of horses and the abandonment of those foals in Assateague. The most pressing matter is that my co-worker, Chip and our friend Kaylee are through the woods. Chip's in need of medical treatment."

The deputy follows me as I begin to walk. Another deputy has Mike. He's sitting in the back seat of the squad car. I notice that the deputy has his windows down, even though it's a little above the freezing mark.

The deputy has figured where we were dumped, and the ambulance leaves proceeding down the road. We arrive at the same time as the ambulance. Kaylee's holding Chip who's unconscious. The emergency technicians start working on Chip, who's placed on a stretcher in the back of the ambulance. Kaylee and I get into the ambulance too and watch the emergency team work on him. Kaylee looks relieved. We're on our way to Shore Memorial Hospital.

Jodi's cell rings and she reads the text message. She gives out a hands-up and everybody looks at her.

"Gertrude, your daughter has been located along with the others. They're on their way to Shore Memorial Hospital. Greg and Kirk take these two and book them for kidnapping, animal neglect and abandonment and talk with the Commonwealth attorney to see if there are any other charges. We need to throw the book at them. I'm going to take Gertrude to the hospital and get statements from Kaylee, Chip and Francie. We'll do a line up later."

Sal Rigatoni and Vince Belli are escorted from Sundial Books. Jodi and Gertrude leave and Jon and Jane breathe a sigh of relief.

"How about if we take Sergeant and Bella for a nice long walk and call it a day?" Jon says as he gives Jane a big bear hug.

"I agree." Jane gives her husband a kiss and Bella yowls. "Ok, guys...we're going for a long walk and if all is well with Francie, you're going home tonight."

As Jon is locking the door, warm air flows north along Main Street. Across the street the marquee has been changed. This week's movie, *The Twilight Saga; Breaking Dawn Part I.*

"Did you notice that the Roxy's showing *Breaking Dawn?*"

"No, I'm in a state of shock. That's all we need is a bunch of vampires and werewolves arriving in Chincoteague."

"I don't think so, Jane. It's too sunny and there's a leash law."

"What would I ever do without your humor, love?"

"You'd have a dull and boring life."

"I'll take dull and for today boring."

Sergeant and Bella are happy for playtime as they're in search of ducks, cats and tourists. A distant siren is heard and Bella stops, scoots her head to the sky and howls.

"Perhaps Bella has some wolf in her!" Jane laughs as she blows a kiss to Jon.

It's Tuesday, and lucky for me, it's not my birthday and it isn't snowing. The alarm has just awakened me and Sergeant and Bella want to go outside, and of course Sophie's causing me to trip as I walk to get her a morning dish of tuna. As usual, nobody gives me a moment to gather my thoughts.

It's been six months since I almost met my demise again. Sometimes I feel like a cat with nine lives. I don't know where to start, so I'll pick up from my release from Shore Memorial Hospital. The next few days are a blur. I was released and mom spent the next week with me. In a way it was a drag. No pot smoking. Mom, Kaylee, Chip and I spent a lot of time being interviewed by Jodi and her ex-partner, Andy. We were able to identify Sal Rigatoni and Vince Belli as our kidnappers. Their partners, twins Marty and Mike Griffin, Sal and Vince were charged with horse abuse and neglect and animal abandonment too. Mike was additionally charged with assault and battery of his fiancée, Brittany who appeared in court smiling and wearing her large diamond ring.

Sally-Sue Moon and Juney Bea Karring are no longer friends. I happened to be observing court proceedings relative to Sal Rigatoni and Vince Belli. My two ex-co-workers were in the crowd also. Sally-Sue was charged with possession of stolen property and was given a court appointed attorney. She had a large outburst in court when Sal Rigatoni's name was called. Sally-Sue started screaming "It's him!" She was led from the court room, is sitting in the county jail, and held without bail. A court date has been scheduled in July, just before pony penning.

Juney Bea Karring was charged with drunken driving, failure to stop at a red light and possession of stolen property. She has a court appointed attorney and her hearing's scheduled the same day as her not-friend. I've heard that Juney Bea hasn't spoken a word to Sally-Sue since they were arrested. They're sharing a cell. Space is limited.

Sal Rigatoni was charged with four counts of kidnapping, horse abuse and neglect, and aggravated assault and battery. He has a hotshot attorney from New Jersey that's able to practice law in Virginia since he's a graduate of the University of Richmond, T.C. Williams School of Law. Sal's trial is scheduled for August.

His cousin, Vince Belli has a court appointed attorney. He's up for the same charges, however; his cousin, Sal isn't sharing his attorney and any money. So much for Italian family togetherness and love. Both remain in jail as Judge Longest wouldn't permit them free on bond due to the severity of their charges. They're big flight risks. God knows that they would run to New Jersey and get lost on the boardwalk of Atlantic City or Asbury Park, never to be seen again, well, on second thought, maybe seen again during this summer with Snooki on *Jersey Shore*.

Warren McKinney was honored by our mayor, Jack Tarr, for his diligence when planning the care and protection for Premarin mares as was Dr. Russell who saved many. Three shifts per day were organized by Doug Fields, mostly manned by Salt Water Cowboys, who cared for, and pampered the neglected horses. As the mares gained strength, some were adopted by our cowboys. Those remaining are to be auctioned next month during pony penning. The four foals survived and live at Elizabeth Allen's farm. Elizabeth and Russ are dating. What has happened with Elizabeth's plans to marry James Parker, who will be released from jail in a few weeks, is a mystery. She's happy, helping Russ with his blacksmith business and taking care of her farm and her four very spoiled yearlings.

Rick LaSlick returned to the Eastern Shore after narrowly escaping recognition from Sal Rigatoni. He stayed in New Orleans for about two months with his parents. His mother and father have remained together, as his mother forgot why she left in the first place. Rick placed twenty-four hour care within the home, to supervise his mother's wandering. Much to Rick's dismay, his mother remembers her travels to Virginia and continues to think that he's married to Gertrude and that they are expecting their first child. She hasn't mentioned Frances Benjamin Johnston, which is a good thing for Rick. When Rick returned to Bullbegger, he asked Beth to come over for dinner, and popped the question. They plan to have a September wedding. Rick's days of lust, gambling and a risky lifestyle are behind him. They plan to have a Catholic wedding and have lots of children.

Kaylee and Chip have been inseparable. Chip recently leased his apartment and moved into Kaylee's condo. I think wedding bells are in the breeze. Chip's a pleasure to share an office with and has a dog, a part-wolf, part-hound named, Eclipse.

And then there's me. Having escaped death with the Eastern Shore Wind Chime Killer, and these New Jersey thugs, I'm happy to be alive. I'm relieved that Jodi told Sally-Sue that an investigation would not ensue about the contents of the Biscotti jar. Sometimes things are better left unsaid.

Since today's Tuesday morning, Jane's having her children's book reading time. I'm ready for some nurturing and so are Sergeant and Bella. We enter a little bit late. About ten island kids are intently listening to a children's book, *Cowboy Dreams*. Bella sits next to Amy, her girlfriend who always wears a pink bow in her hair, and Sergeant takes his seat next to Jake, a usually rambunctious three year old. Sergeant usually steals one of Jake's toys within minutes. Jake will begin to cry and story time will be interrupted.

Nobody is crying and the dogs are behaving as I walk past Jane. She has the patience of a saint. I continue walking to the back porch. Today is warm and sunny. As I sit in a wicker rocker looking at the dock, and Chincoteague Bay listening to Jane, I realize that this is exactly where I need to be. In the background, Jane's soothing voice is heard, reading to the island kids. "When I was a girl I wanted to be a cowboy. My earliest memories are of lying on the living room rug, listening to "The Lone Ranger" on the radio. "Hi Ho, Silver! Away!" were practically the first words I ever said."

I'm a year older, don't know if I'm wiser, however; content after all it isn't Monday and it's not hot, foggy, buggy or rainy. Best of all it's not snowing and it's Tuesday and Jane's having story time. Life on Chincoteague Island doesn't get much better than this.

Acknowledgements

http://exxonmobil.com/Corporate/enery.climate_con_veh
icle_algae.aspx

http://en.wikipedia.org/wiki/Ron_Jeremy

https://friendsofanimals.org/programs/domestic-
feral/horses/drugpmu.html

https://www.friendsofanimals.org/programs/domestic-
feral/horses/pmu.html

http://premarin.org

Babiak, Paul, Ph.D and Hare, Robert D., Ph.D, *Snakes in
Suites When Psychopaths Go To Work,* Regan Books,
HarperCollins Publishers Inc. New York, New York 10022,
2006

Khalsa, Dayal Kaur, *Cowboy Dreams,* Clarkson N. Potter,
Inc./Publishers New York, 1990

Mariner, Kirk: *Off 13 The Eastern Shore of Virginia
Guidebook,* Miona Publications New Church, Virginia
23415, 2002

Mariner, Kirk: *True Tales of the Eastern Shore*, Miona Publications New Church, Virginia 23415, 2003

Tennyson, Noel: *The Lady's Chair and the Ottoman,* Lothrop, Lee & Shepard Books, New York, 1987

Zona, Guy A: *The Soul Would Have No Rainbow if the Eyes Had No Tears and Other Native American Proverbs*, Simon and Schuster, 1994

Books by Teresa Adele Bettino

The Adventures of Sugarbabe and Thunder

The Ten Commandments of a Welfare Worker

Degen and Me

The Cats of Hanover Juvenile Correctional Center

Unique Shadows

A Wicker Rocker

Two Dogs and a Boy

Wind Chimes

Teresa Adele Bettino was born in East Orange New Jersey. A retired social worker, Teresa resides with her family in Mechanicsville, Virginia.

Partial proceeds from book sales will be donated to animal rescue.

Photo:

Courtesy Nancy Wilmink

www.ingramcontent.com/pod-product-compliance
Lightning Source LLC
Chambersburg PA
CBHW061151170626
46809CB00003B/1051